*Amy Madden*

# Amy Madden

## J. Boyett

SALTIMBANQUE BOOKS

NEW YORK

For Leo.

## BY THE SAME AUTHOR

## Acknowledgments

As usual, Kelly Kay Griffith provided valuable input into earlier drafts of this book.

And thank you to Mary Sheridan.

*Amy Madden*

# One

A spark of consciousness strangled out by thick green tentacles like snakes, and then by something even more snake-like than that. Meanwhile, Bud sat alone on his deck, in his backyard. Looking at his pool. The water was nice but there was no one in it. On the metal lawn table before him rested his can of Coke. He kind of wanted a beer but it wasn't even eight in the morning; about two hours ago he'd jerked awake from an unremembered dream. He'd stayed in bed a while, partly because it was still awful early on a Saturday morning but also because he had a feeling that, good or bad, it had been a stirring dream.

A big house. Way too expensive for a town like Hutchins, but on the other hand too luxurious for a town like Hutchins, as well. It had a fireplace; he didn't expect to use it much because it also had central heating and air, but he figured once he managed to get a girl over he would stoke it up. (It was gas, so he wouldn't have to figure out firewood or any of that stuff.) It had a big kitchen with countertops made from some kind of stone; he didn't remember right now what kind it was, but when he'd been buying the place a couple months ago the real estate lady had said it was impressive. It had enough rooms for him to raise a few kids here, if he ever decided he had any interest in doing so. And the pool out back, with a deck. Right now its water lay still in the windless morning. Not a creature stirred, unless they were too small to see. Only the dull sound of the occasional passing car a few blocks over gave any sign of life.

The place took a hell of a mortgage. Bud could afford it with what FlashComm paid him. Anyway, the mortgage would have been higher elsewhere—the house's luxury was mitigated by the

3

fact that nobody wanted to move to Hutchins. Most of the other houses in this ambitious new development remained empty. All of them, in fact, as far as Bud knew. A prefab deluxe ghost town.

The house had been a stupid expense. But moving to Hutchins had made him feel like a loser. The town incarnated the kind of boring, middling suburbia he'd spent his youth, and his twenties, vowing to get away from. No matter how much FlashComm paid him, accepting the job and moving here represented a defeat. He'd tried to prove it was actually a step up by buying the fanciest house he could.

Besides, he'd assumed having a fancy house with a pool would get him laid. But none of the few college girls he'd dared try to chat up had expressed any interest in fucking him. Not even when he slipped his pool into the conversation.

Ah, well. He'd only recently moved to town.

He continued to gaze out at his yard. He hadn't noticed till after he'd bought the place, but the fences were so low that even if he did manage to lure a coed over for a little poolside poontang, they wouldn't have any privacy. Not that it mattered, since no one else lived in any of the equally big, flashy houses surrounding his. Bud was all alone on his chilly, empty deck, staring at his huge quiet pool. He took another swallow of his Coke.

The doorbell rang. Bud had the back door open, so he heard the bell clear as if he'd been in the house. He jumped, sloshing Coke onto his hand, and twisted around to stare over his shoulder. Unlikely to be good news, early in the morning like this. Not like he had any friends.

He hadn't heard a car pull up. And yet no one went anywhere in Hutchins except by car. Eerie.

A voice called, "Yo, Bud! Hey, Bud, you there?"

Bud blinked. That sounded like his cousin Cory. Impossible, since Cory lived hundreds of miles away. It took him a second to untangle the mystery—Cory must, in fact, be here, in Hutchins. Bud heaved himself up out of his chair and went inside.

"Dude, check out your *house!*" cried Cory when Bud opened the door. Cory reached up on his tiptoes to give the bigger man a bear hug, which was awkward because of Cory's huge rucksack. He squeezed past Bud through the doorway—also awkward, again thanks to the rucksack, and so Cory let the encumbrance drop to the floor with a massive thump as he wandered into the living room, head tilted back and eyes and jaw wide as if stumbling without warning into St. Peter's Basilica.

Good ol' Cory, with his floppy brown mop of hair, with his frame that was small yet, considering that he did so much drinking and drugging and never exercised, weirdly fit. Except, well, Bud supposed lugging rucksacks all over the country should count as exercise. He frowned at the one Cory had just dumped on his floor. The thing seemed suspiciously full. "So, cuz," said Bud. "What's up? Just passing through?"

The face Cory turned on Bud seemed honestly surprised. "You didn't get my letter?"

"Your *letter*? No, man, I don't think I've gotten a *letter* from anyone in my whole life."

"I mean my e-mail. You didn't get my e-mail?"

"Nah, dude."

"You *sure* you didn't get it? The one I sent about staying here maybe?"

"Nah, dude."

Cory put his hands on his hips. He looked really puzzled. "I was sure you got it," he muttered.

"Well, did I write you back? If I'd gotten it I would have written you back."

"I *think* you did."

"No, Cory."

"Well, anyway.... You don't care if I crash here a few days, do you? There's a festival going on nearby, and you're the only person I know who lives anywhere *near* Hutchins. And besides, you got mad space, bro!"

"A festival? In Hutchins?"

As Cory started talking about the festival, Bud's interest flagged. It was something to do with crystals, and there was going to be folk music and techno. Plus it wasn't actually in

Hutchins, but about thirty miles further out into the sticks, in some little town. When Bud asked the name of the town Cory didn't even remember exactly; Bud inwardly rolled his eyes.

Well, whatever. Why make a fuss? He'd been bored and lonely. He was glad Cory had popped up, although he was careful not to say so, because he didn't want to have to eat his words later when Cory started driving him nuts.

He clapped his hand on his cousin's shoulder. "C'mon, you hungry? Let's go to Denny's and get some breakfast." It went without saying that Bud would pay.

# Two

In some ways it was fun hanging out with Cory. Though they were very different, they'd always gotten along; they hadn't seen each other in more than a year and it was fun to catch up.

But Cory didn't have a car, and Hutchins had no public bus service, so the guys were pretty much stuck with each other. It started to get old. After a couple hours, Bud was nostalgic for his lonely morning and thinking about how relaxing it would be to binge-watch TV all weekend, if only he didn't have to babysit his cousin. And then there was the bullshit Cory spouted; the guy got worse every year. He kept talking about aliens and mothmen and all sorts of amazing crap.

The best thing to do with a houseguest like Cory was get drunk together. Even if you didn't actually believe him about all the wonders of New Age pseudoscience, the stuff became more fun to listen to.

Bud didn't want to start drinking at noon, though. From mid-morning to early afternoon he drove Cory around on a guided tour of Hutchins. They didn't go anyplace worth getting out of the vehicle for. Bud didn't find the mall much more attractive than his car; in his car at least he could control the music. And he didn't feel like sharing with Cory his affection for the local cemetery. So they went home for a couple hours. Bud had assumed they'd watch TV to kill time till dinner, but Cory waxed disdainful of TV's spiritually deadening properties, and insisted they sit on the sofa and just talk. He went on long monologues about the stuff he was into, then would ask Bud what he thought of it all. Bud would shrug and try to be polite as he explained that, no, he didn't believe in alchemy, and so forth.

"That's because of all that computer programming," said Cory at one point, nodding sagely. "It's got you thinking you can fit the whole world into little numbers and boxes. But sometimes the universe jumps out and *grabs* you, man!"

Finally, four o'clock arrived. Bud figured that was late enough to propose treating Cory at Old Petey's. He wondered what he would do with Cory till the first day of the festival, which was Friday (suggesting to Bud that its organizers had not even bothered to consider the possibility that some of the attendees might be people with regular jobs).

"How are you going to get to this festival, anyway?" asked Bud. "I can't take you, I'm working."

"Relax, bro—it'll just happen."

Old Petey's Tavern was part of a strip mall complex, the listless stores lined up in a row like prisoners waiting to be shot. But Old Petey's was not actually part of the strip itself: the strip mall had an unusually big parking lot, big enough to accommodate Petey's, which sat in its own building thirty yards from the line of stores. Bud didn't know how long the place had been there, with its dark rustic-looking wood siding and its charming rocking chair chained to the railing; not much longer than his own brand-new development, he would guess. Inside, the walls were painted a log-cabin umber. The laminated menus had been printed with a down-home sort of font, and touted fare like burgers, meatloaf, and California rolls. Bud walked past the hostess and led Cory straight to the horseshoe bar. The bartender nodded as he handed them each a menu.

Cory was looking around with a wrinkled mouth. "This place is cool," Bud assured him with a murmur. Sort of pleading. Hopefully his cousin wouldn't alienate the staff at Old Petey's, the only bar in the vicinity of his house that lay along relatively straight, tranquil roads. The trouble with going out and getting trashed in a town like Hutchins was that afterward you had to drive home.

They ordered some beers and burgers—Cory got a veggie burger—and Cory quit talking philosophy and began to pump Bud about his own life. Bud told a few stories about work and tried to make them funny. He had to occasionally pause and contextualize things for Cory by explaining some facet of corporate culture.

Bud nursed his beer, because he wanted this outing to last long enough that he could credibly go to bed at the end of it, but he didn't want to drink so much that he got them killed during the drive home. By the time he was ready to order his second beer, Cory was ordering his third. The place had gotten more active. At some point a pair of girls had sat at the bar three stools down from Cory, two stacked blondes. Bud hadn't noticed their arrival; odd, given their supernatural degree of hotness. He tried to engineer a relatively loud conversation about his own high-paying job and swimming pool, and steer the talk away from Cory and his weird, ignorant, and embarrassing preoccupations.

But goddam if those hot girls weren't into alchemy. They scooted down, presumably drawn by Cory's festival talk. They listened with uncanny calm, as if from a great height; Bud found the effect intimidating and arousing. The blondes looked enough alike that by squinting at them you could imagine they were twins, if you were into that. Yet they were *not* actually twins, which meant you could masturbate to such a fantasy (or, in theory, actually persuade them to have a threesome with you) without worrying about any incestuous ick factor.

One would be plenty, though. And since there was one apiece for him and Cory, Bud developed an anticipatory erection. But the girls seemed only interested in talking about alchemy—or, rather, in listening to Cory hold forth about it.

Bud tried joining in. After all, he was an okay-looking guy; he'd always thought his neck reminiscent of Mel Gibson's, and in this shirt his slight man-boobs could pass for pecs. His face was too round and his brown hair was already thinning at thirty years old, but he wasn't *that* bad. But he just couldn't bring himself to fake a belief in alchemy. So he tried to pass himself off as the skeptical yet open-minded voice of reason, once in a while raising a finger and introducing some query in a gentlemanly, devil's-advocate kind of way. That had to be harmless enough, he figured—these girls just had to at least be open to the idea that the physical universe did not run on magic.

Yet every time he raised one of his increasingly-timid objections, the girls barely let their eyes flutter his way. Cory would answer his objection, with patient wise confidence.

Bud tried to be cool. Not slobber, at least. No that he cared much about his own dignity. He just knew that if he didn't act cool, even the infinitesimal chance he did have at fucking one of these girls would disappear.

And he did want to fuck one of them. Nothing new about that—except that he *really* wanted to fuck them. It wasn't even a matter of his usual horniness. More like there was something special about them, the girls. Not in some pussy romantic sense. They just emanated some sort of very powerful vibe. Bud didn't believe in that kind of thing, but he nevertheless felt it. Maybe this was, like, charisma? The whole bar just felt more charged now that they'd shown up, more alive.

He ordered a third beer. Neither Cory nor the two girls were paying any attention to him anymore, but it wouldn't do to turn aside from the conversation altogether, to leave them to it while he stared off in another direction; that would make him look like a sore, sullen loser.

Bud imagined trying to go to sleep while in the guest bedroom Cory had a noisy threesome with the stacked blonde almost-twins. After the sex Cory and the girls would cool off by skinny-dipping in Bud's pool.

Much as he tried to keep looking at Cory's endlessly talking mouth—no easy feat, since Cory's head was turned away from Bud toward the girls—and keep seeming interested, it got to be too disheartening. His attention drifted to the beer mug in front of him.

*If only alchemy were real,* he thought, *I could turn my shit life into gold.*

Loosened by the alcohol, his eyes slid around to the other side of the bar. There, he caught another cute blonde looking at him. When their eyes met, both dropped their gazes, blushing.

10

Bud snuck his eyes back up to look at her again. She stared self-consciously into space. Alone? Surely she was here with a boyfriend or a date who'd just popped into the bathroom. But there wasn't a drink or a coaster at the place beside her. She actually wasn't *that* great, not stunning like the two wannabe alchemists, but cute in a girl-next-door-but-with-spunk kind of way. Her wavy yellow hair was poofy, and came down a little past her shoulders. She wore a pink T-shirt tucked into her jeans.

Maybe she really had come by herself. Bud did that sometimes, after all. Maybe she had come in the hopes of meeting someone....

The whole time Bud was looking at her, he felt sure she felt his gaze. Then she confirmed the vibe by turning his way and smiling. A shy smile; but she'd clearly known she would find him already looking at her.

Bud's first, humiliated impulse was to break eye contact. He reminded himself that such habits were the main reason no woman had ever yet lain eyes on that pool of his. He forced himself to smile back, in what he hoped was a natural, friendly way.

She really was pretty, he realized. You just didn't notice how much at first, because she seemed so normal. And he could tell that under that pink T-shirt her tits were pretty good.

It would be a heinous waste to not go chat up a cute girl that he'd already gotten to smile at him. He turned to Cory and his two acolytes, planning to tell them he was going to slip away for a second. But he couldn't even catch any of their six eyes. So Bud turned back away from them, planning to go to the pink-shirt girl. But someone else caught his eye before he could.

Another woman sitting at the bar, on the other side of the horseshoe. Looking at him. Not the way the smiling pretty girl had been—this woman was frowning, scowling, her brow pinched and mouth puckered, her head tilted as if she were puzzled and trying to figure out what to make of Bud.

Not a hot girl. More like a central-casting librarian from an old movie. Sixtyish? Fiftyish? Drab clothes that afterwards he wouldn't be able to remember very well. He tried smiling at her, as if he hadn't noticed her googly-eyed stare.

She slid her froggy eyes to the pretty girl, looking back and forth between her and Bud. The girl had looked at Bud again. Her worried grimace told him that she'd noticed his discomfort.

Bud turned back to the alchemy discussion, unable to imagine trying to mac on the girl in the older woman's presence. Maybe if he waited a few minutes, just nonchalantly acted like he was into the New Age discussion Cory was leading, then the older woman would go to the bathroom or something and he could make his move.

But he knew he was fucking up. Pussying out. Like always! He should be trying to score. No one but himself could make him stop being a loser.

He tried to sneak another glance at the cute girl. Engage in a bit more eye contact. But his gaze got snagged again by that frog-eyed lady.

Space seemed to bend in front of him, or maybe it was the light bending and all of a sudden refracting funny. Of course, actually the bend must be in his own brainwaves, bending his thoughts into some painful distortion. Bud squeezed shut his eyes, ducked his head, massaged his temples. Too much cheap beer—he ought to switch to more expensive stuff. When he blinked his eyes back open, both women from the other side of the bar were gone. He managed to catch sight of the cute girl, walking out the front door. As for the old frog-eyed lady, not a trace.

# Three

The bizarre exchange of glances with the cute girl and the googly-eyed woman left Bud so rattled and disappointed that he drank more than he'd planned. When the bartender handed him his sixth pint, he was a little offended—didn't the guy know Bud had to drive home? Didn't he care if Bud lived or died? Shouldn't Bud have been cut off by now?

When it came time for Bud to pay the tab, he and Cory were tied at eight pints. The hot almost-twins gave Bud a look when he took out his wallet. Or he thought they did, he was too blitzed to really judge. Anyway, he experienced their gaze as a cool assumption that he would pay their tab, as well. So he did.

At least they didn't accompany the guys back to Bud's house in order to have sex with his cousin. Cory did say he'd invited them to the festival on Friday.

"Don't they have jobs?" he asked Cory, during the drive back home.

Cory shrugged, as if to say that things like jobs were easily taken care of.

The houses were dark as their car crept along the road home, dark and a little swimmy in Bud's intoxicated vision. Both guys were subdued: dulled by drink, plus Bud had to concentrate extra hard on the road, plus Cory was probably worn out from the hours of talking to those two beautiful girls. Cory said, "Yo, dude, doesn't it ever depress you? Living in this, like, ghost neighborhood?"

Bud sighed. "It's not so bad," he said. "It's just new. Other people will move in. Eventually."

"At least a ghost town is someplace that people already *left*," Cory said. "You live someplace where nobody ever even bothered to come."

Back at the house, Cory asked if Bud was sure he didn't want to watch TV or anything (he'd reached the level of intoxication at which brain-deadening TV waves became acceptable), but didn't argue when Bud said he'd rather just go to bed. Even though it was only a little after ten, they had been drinking for six hours.

Bud showed Cory to the guest bedroom. Cory was amazed to find the bed already made: "Are you, like, expecting company all the time, cuz?"

Nope. Bud was never expecting company.

Although Bud really was tired from all the drinking, and from the long day with Cory, once back in his room he found himself still too jittery to sleep. Plus his stomach felt funny. He suddenly realized that all those beers were mixing together with his burger to form a particularly gnarly shit. Since the brew was still percolating, it didn't seem worth it to go to bed yet.

One of Bud's two laptops was here in the bedroom with him. Bud decided he could watch some porn or something until he was ready to go to the bathroom, or till he felt relaxed enough to try to sleep. He hunted around for earbuds, since he had just told Cory that he didn't want to watch TV with him and didn't want to come off as a dick by having the noise of some video emanating from behind his door. He didn't see any, though. Whatever, fuck it. He'd just keep the volume low.

At first he typed in the url for pornhub.com and tried to find a threesome with a couple of blonde girls, to make up for the double-whammy disappointment of the almost-twins, followed by the disappearing cute girl. But out of the first fifty videos, the only two-blonde threesome was with a black guy, and Bud had a hard time imagining himself in the place of the dude if the dude was black. He kept scrolling through the thumbnail images till he found a POV blow job being given by a tattooed chick with purple hair. It was only the one girl, and Bud preferred at least two, but she was pretty hot. Bud set the sound real low and started the video. After a few minutes of trying to jerk off, though, he realized it wasn't going to work. He could only manage a weak erection. What with his bubbling indigestion, his drunkenness, and his depression, making himself cum would be work, if he even managed it at all. So he closed the porno and looked for something else to watch, something that wouldn't require viewer participation.

He went on Netflix, clicking around for streaming Fantasy and Sci-Fi movies. He didn't really give a shit what he watched. Preferably nothing good, so he wouldn't feel obligated to keep watching once he got too sleepy, or after he'd taken his shit.

There was a movie that looked like it took place in dungeons and shit, and starred a bunch of warlocks or whatever. He clicked on that one. Weirdly, it seemed to start right in the middle of a scene, without any preliminary credits. Maybe they came a little later. Whatever. Bud watched it without much interest, merely as something to take his mind off his weariness.

The scene was indeed in some sort of dungeon. Like, a subterranean cave, with flames leaping and licking up from behind orange outcroppings of rock. As far as Bud could tell, those open flames were the only sources of light, although everything was a little brighter and clearer than if that had really been the case. Plainly, a bit of studio trickery at work. Maybe the scene took place in hell.

It couldn't be a dungeon, exactly, because no one was chained up. Only a few people in the scene. Most of them were sort of idling, standing around in brown tunics, generically peasantish. Sitting at something like a desk—a big table, anyway—was a grotesque, wizened old man in a robe and cowl, making notations on a long scroll with a big, dirty plume. He gave Bud the impression of being an apothecary. Except just how the fuck did one give the impression of being an apothecary? Maybe by being surrounded by bottles and potions, but there was no such set dressing here. With the volume so low, the dialogue and sound effects all dribbled in only a bit above the threshold of audibility. Bud leaned in close to the screen, concentrating, listening hard, trying to follow the scene.

The apothecary squinted up at him with an unkind smirk. "Well? Yes?" the old man wheezed. His flesh seemed not merely aged; its laxness seemed the result of rot and decay. "Can I help you? What have you got?"

Bud looked around at all the other guys in the chamber. Suddenly they all seemed more removed from the apothecary's desk than they had before, as if they were giving him space. Still, Bud said, "I think all these people were here first."

The apothecary flung his hand dismissively. "What have you got, what have you got?!" he croaked, and stood and came around the desk to put his moist cold palm flat against Bud's belly. Bud forced himself not to recoil, even though the apothecary had his hand pretty dang low on Bud's abdomen. "Ooo, good, good!" the old man cackled, palpitating the flesh almost but not quite painfully with his fingers. "Yes, we can make use of that."

Looking down, Bud remembered he was naked. He was mortified to see how shriveled and small his penis was. How cold.

The apothecary was leading him away; "Come, come," he clucked. He led him by the hand, which was creepy and inappropriate, but Bud followed without protest. They passed close by a couple of fires, but they didn't warm Bud up—in fact, cold seemed to emanate from them instead of heat, and Bud felt that, if he'd plunged his hand into one of those flames, it would be freezing enough to burn.

"Um." Bud wasn't sure he was allowed to speak, but he risked it. "Um, excuse me, sir. Where are we headed?"

The apothecary whipped around to grin at him. It was disorienting, because the apothecary's face was suddenly super-close to Bud's, and also because they didn't stop walking. The apothecary was walking backwards now, his head so close that it blocked Bud's view of where they were going. The rotting old man put his hand on Bud's abdomen again. This time it really was right above the groin, the old man's wormy fingers tickling in his pubic hair, and Bud felt his testicles and penis shrinking even further up into his body, hiding from the cold of the old man's touch.

"What will you do with all that mud in there?" hissed the old man, giving his belly another squeeze. His breath didn't smell exactly bad, but vaguely unsettling: like chilled mushrooms. "But *she* can make use of it."

Bud felt it would be impolite to pry. Yet he couldn't help it: "Really? What will she do?"

"One man's shit," said the apothecary, "is another woman's gold."

At those words, pain ripped through Bud's bowels. He cried out, and would have gone down on his knees had the apothecary's hands not suddenly been under his armpits to yank him back upright. "Up, up!" the clammy man yelped. "Time to get up and report for dinner!"

It was not merely the sudden pain that had almost forced him to his knees. Bud was heavier now. Specifically, his abdomen was heavier, as if he were carrying around some great mass in his guts.

The apothecary rapped his knuckles on Bud's belly. They made a heavy dull flesh-muffled sound. Bud howled and doubled over.

The apothecary laughed, good-naturedly enough, but without much patience. "Up, up, up, up! Don't you want to get your gold?!"

"No," moaned Bud. "No, I don't want to."

"What!" shouted the apothecary, faking surprise, just barely disguising his grin. "What, you don't want me to cut you open and pull it out?! You could get a goodly sum for all that treasure!"

"No!" howled Bud. "No, it hurts, and I'm scared!"

The apothecary tut-tutted. "What a disappointment, what a disappointment! So you want it changed back?"

"Yes! Yes!"

"Well, no one'll do *that*, I'm afraid. Where will you find anyone so foolish as to turn gold *back* into shit? But *she* may be able to make a change into something more to her liking, if we ask her nicely. Iron, say."

Bud wanted to object that iron would be even heavier and more painful than gold, but nothing came out but agonized cries, and it was all he could do to keep his footing as the apothecary dragged him along.

Almost as if the apothecary had heard Bud's unspoken objection, he said, "Now, *I* of course lack the art to make this pleasant for you. If I should make such a change—which I do have the skill for, mind you!—but if I should make such a change, it would not be pleasant. I'm not in the business of making things pleasant even for me, hee hee! Oh, but she can, *she* can! When she wants to! Ha!"

The apothecary was a madman. Bud had failed to notice that till now, because the guy was so much more powerful than he was.

"Now here we come!" he was saying. "Here's the bit you want!"

As the apothecary spoke, Bud became aware for the first time that the area around him *felt* different, somehow. Maybe it was the air pressure, or a shift in temperature, or a subtle change in the lighting, the gloom shot through with occasional gleams. He was in a new space. Despite the chewing agony in his gut, he made himself raise his head and look up. It took a few seconds of blinking through the smear of pain for him to put together what he was seeing.

At some point they'd passed out of the claustrophobic hellish chamber into a huge hellish chamber. Only the darkness and a sense of great weight hanging overhead told Bud that they were still inside; the ceiling of this cavern stretched high out of sight. In the distance off to his left and right cold yellow flames still spurted from the rock. Ahead of him rose a sheer subterranean mountain wall. Something illuminated it, though he couldn't tell what—couldn't be the flames, they were too small and far away.

What he saw upon that great, huge wall was something like a gate. Stretched around that gate, encompassing it, was a gigantic horseshoe magnet, blood-red and dully glowing, a monstrous version of the magnets in old-fashioned cartoons. That upside-down magnet had to be at least twelve stories tall. Even though Bud registered its goofiness, it was too big for him to laugh at, even if he hadn't been in such pain.

Now he realized that it wasn't a gate that the magnet stretched over like a brooding dark rainbow. Or, if it was a gate, it was a very special type, one cast in the form of a dark gray iron vagina, maybe nine stories high to the magnet's twelve.

Somehow, while gaping at the magnet and the vagina, Bud had forgotten about the apothecary. Now the rotted old man popped into Bud's face, fingers back on his belly. "See?" he leered. "Let *her* change it, and maybe it won't hurt so much."

It occurred to Bud that it still sort of looked like it was the apothecary changing it, since it was his hand, but he got it that this time the rotted old man was using power bequeathed in some unseen way by "her," whoever she was. And then he could feel the transformation take place, and certainly it was very different from before, when the apothecary had changed his shit into gold. He *knew*, somehow, that that gold had now been transformed into iron, he understood in some instinctive way that that was the change that had been effected in his guts. But there was no agony this time—far from it. This time, he felt the added mass of the iron, so much heavier than gold, as merely one satisfying aspect of a wave of pleasure rippling through his center, emanating out his extremities.

Not only that, but he felt his middle drawn toward that vagina gate—or, he supposed, technically it was drawn toward that strange magnet arching over the pudenda. That must be because she'd changed the gold shit into iron. And that must be why the metal in his belly didn't hurt anymore. When it had been just gold, he'd had to bear the whole weight of the metal lump by himself. His innards were too soft and delicate for that, they'd probably gotten torn up, he'd be lucky not to be ruptured permanently.

But now that it was not gold but iron (which he suddenly realized was the more valuable substance by simple virtue of the fact that apparently she wanted it), he didn't have to hold up that weight at all. It no longer dragged him down, but was pulling him forward. He could have tried holding it *back*, if he'd wanted to—but why? The invisible tugging was not remotely uncomfortable—far from it—it was deeply pleasurable, in fact it was far and away the loveliest physical pleasure he'd ever known—it was like the sweetest sexual stroke he could ever know, slowed down and down and down to the most voluptuous slowness, as the soft strength of the horseshoe magnet drew him along by his middle ever closer and closer to the iron vagina gate....

"Dude, what're you doing?"

Bud blinked, jarred by that voice he couldn't yet place. He blinked some more as his eyes tried to take in surroundings that he knew he recognized, but which felt like they'd been unseen for a billion years.

After a few seconds it clicked: this was his living room. He was standing buck naked in his living room with all the lights out, arms outstretched, feet planted far apart, jutting his pelvis toward the TV as if there were a cord connecting his dick to the screen.

Again, Cory's voice from behind him: "What're you *doing*, dude?"

Bud spun his head around to look back over his shoulder at Cory, not thinking yet to drop his outstretched arms. Cory stood in his underwear at the corner of the hallway, as if he'd been on his way to the kitchen for a glass of water but had stopped short when he'd seen Bud standing in the dim room.

Bud turned and looked straight ahead. Instead of the vagina gate, he saw only the dim vague shadow of his own reflection in the flat screen of the TV. He looked down at himself. Not only were his hips jutting forward; his penis was erect. Not merely erect, but super-erect, as if the most beautiful invisible woman who'd ever lived were squeezing his dick and leading him forward by it. That was how good it felt, he realized, now that he paused long enough to notice.

Cory was circling around him, giving him a wide berth. Bud was too dazed to think to cover himself in time, and when Cory circled around far enough to see the pulsing hard-on he jerked to a halt. "Dude," he said, with a hint of reproachful distaste.

Bud had just enough time to be thankful that, if Cory had to see his penis at all, he was seeing it in this abnormally impressive state. Then, without really even getting to completely feel it, without being quite entirely reconciled back into his own flesh, he became aware that its pleasure was culminating; he looked back down at his penis in time to see the first blob of semen burst out of it, then the rest stutter and dribble away as the organ quivered and spasmed back down to detumescence.

"Dude," Cory said again, with a subtle variation in tone.

Bud hadn't recovered enough to feel embarrassment yet, though he could sense it approaching through his numbness. But first came a churning metamorphosis in his guts. He jackknifed over with a cry, and heard and smelled something savage as it tore at him inside and he felt shit sliding down the backs of his thighs.

*"Dude,"* said Cory. "Do you want me to get a doctor?!"

"I'm fine. Just not feeling good."

"Well, yeah, dude, that's why I would get the doctor."

"No, please. Please. I'm fine. Just a little embarrassed. Please don't tell anyone about this."

Cory sounded almost tender as he said, "Aw, no, dude, don't be embarrassed. Anyway, who would I tell?"

*Those two beautiful almost-twins,* thought Bud. He became aware of a noise—like people having sex, three of them. "What is that noise?" he asked.

Cory turned sheepish. "Yeah," Cory slowly and reluctantly said. "That's kind of what woke me up. Was that you have your porno so loud."

Bud felt dizzy. He wanted to explain that there hadn't been a porno, he'd been watching that movie … but then he remembered he hadn't actually been watching the movie, he'd been *in* it, him and the apothecary. *A dream,* he marveled. *Everything after I opened pornhub and started scrolling through thumbnails must have been a dream.* Judging from the soundtrack drifting down from his bedroom, there were three people in the porno, and Bud wondered if even the POV blow job from the tattooed girl had been a dream, if he had clicked on the two-blonde threesome even despite the black guy and everything past that had been a mirage.

He remembered how much pain he'd been in, in the dream, and how the pain had turned to pleasure when he'd given himself up to "her" pull. For some reason he focussed on that as if it were an important lesson.

Cory uncomfortably shifted his weight back and forth from one foot to the other. "Okay, well, uh," he said. "I guess I'm just gonna head back to bed, dude—you look like you can handle yourself fine...."

# Four

The Grandbled Cemetery was an unusually lush, green spot for Hutchins. The grass here lacked the yellow tinge of most grass in this region. Sally squatted and pressed her palm down upon the springy moist dark-green carpet. Grandbled must have a heck of an endowment, to keep itself so pleasant. It was nice, but also a little macabre: laying down a carpet of vibrant sod over the preservatives-pumped corpses beneath.

She rose and continued on her way to the gate and her car. She'd woken up today, vaguely feeling the urge to do something outside her usual routine. Why not visit Grandma's grave? Her early-childhood memories of the funeral were so thin, ghostly. She'd thought that coming here would solidify them. But the sight of the headstone had awakened nothing; instead, she'd started to come down with the creepy feeling that it was the world itself and all its denizens that were wispy and phantasmal.

But the cemetery was a nice stroll, if you weren't in the throes of grief. As she rounded the corner of a large mausoleum she gave a start. Standing a few yards away, looking down at a tombstone with his hands in his pockets, was that guy from the night before, from Old Petey's.

Sally was sure it was him. Kind of cute, even if he could stand to lose a few pounds; but last night's eye-tag had started to feel so awkward that Sally had just left some money on the bar counter and made her escape. Anyway, nothing was ever lost in Hutchins—with a population of forty thousand, the town was small enough that you wound up bumping into everyone else once a year or so. Now her mouth twisted with the irony that they should, in fact, bump into each other the very next day, but that it should be at a cemetery: an even more awkward social situation, and far less conducive to any sort of romantic introductions.... Not that he'd seemed into the idea of actually coming over and saying anything to her, even at Old Petey's....

Except here the guy was, walking toward her, smiling nervously, waving experimentally. Although she wasn't exactly in the mood for this kind of thing right now, Sally pasted a smile on her own face. "Hey," she said.

"Hey," he said, holding out his hand to shake. She took it. "I saw you at Old Petey's last night."

"Yup." She cast around for some way to refer to the night before without being awkward. "You were there with that guy."

A grimace spasmed across the guy's face. "Yeah," he said. "My cousin. Cory."

He clearly didn't want to talk about his cousin. Sour grapes because of how well the cousin had been doing with those tall curvy babes? No doubt Sally'd been second-best, something this guy had decided to settle for ... but she willed herself not to get offended by him before they'd even had their first conversation. He'd merely happened to be present while his cousin chatted up two girls.

"I'm Sally," she said.

"Bud," he said.

There was something endearing about the way he seemed to be always on the verge of tripping over himself. No wonder it had been his cousin chatting up the girls. A player, this guy was not.

"I'm a programmer over at FlashComm," he was saying. "A systems engineer, actually. I have a house over in the Dealy neighborhood."

"Wow. That crazy new development? I thought they'd built all those houses and then realized no one could afford to buy any."

"Yeah, well," he said with a forced little laugh. "It does get a little lonely out there."

Wait. Duh. He'd told her about the house in the Dealy neighborhood to signal how rich he was. "I work at Barnes and Noble," she said.

"Oh?" he said, keeping his face carefully blank.

The careful blankness provoked her. "Yeah. I'm a manager now. Really proud of it."

"Sure, sure ... and plus, you know, it's not, like, forever...."

"Yeah. Thanks. Okay, well, I need to go...."

"No! Hey, wait, hold up."

Sally had been stepping past him back in the direction of her car. She stopped, and watched Bud's face as he cast around for some way to fix his gaffe. His cluelessness, too, was kind of endearing.

"You want to see this thing I was looking at?" he asked.

She nodded, at a loss for what "thing" he might be referring to. As he led her back the way he'd come, she realized it was the tombstone he'd been studying, when she'd spotted him. Carved into the marker was a poem:

SHE CAME, AND WAS OUR DEAREST FRIEND

AND IS NOW IN HEAVEN, WITH LIFE WITHOUT END

According to the dates, the grave was that of a fourteen-year-old girl named Linda Middleton. Dead more than twenty years ago. The guy from Petey's stared at the tombstone, eyebrows drawn, eyes misty. "Isn't that so beautiful and sad?"

"Yeah," said Sally, gently. Her stuck-up bitchiness whispered to her that what was *really* sad was the meter. And sneeringly wanted to know the odds against a fourteen-year-old American girl and her parents being "dearest friends."

Suddenly she did feel sad. Not because of the gravestone. What made her sad was her own cynicism, that couldn't let her stand next to this admittedly awkward guy without shitting on him and his sensitivity. What a miserable bitch she'd turned into, so well-armored against any emotions but boredom and fear. Not to mention the pathetic charade of pretending to be proud of her job at Barnes and Noble!

"It *is* nice," she added, a little insistently.

He nodded, pleased at her agreement. "Do you have, like, a favorite?"

"Huh?"

"Well, like, one in particular that you like to look at. Like, I wander around a lot when I come, but there's a few highlights that I always check out. Like, have you looked at that big mausoleum down on the other end, from the forties? That the guy built for himself, his four sons, and his dog?"

"I guess I just came to visit the grave of my grandma."

Bud looked totally lost. Then he exclaimed, "Oh! You come out here to actually *visit* people!"

"Yes. Why do *you* come here?"

"Just to … just to look around, really. I'm sorry, I'm new here and I just don't know that many interesting places in Hutchins. This cemetery beats the mall, anyway."

"I see," she said. Sally's Barnes and Noble was at the mall. "So your version of going to the mall is to come to the cemetery on a beautiful spring day and read the tombstones of dead kids. Morbid much?"

"Well. But. Yeah, I mean, but, like, *you're* here, too. Right?"

*"For my grandma."*

"Sure, sure," he said, nodding his head like in the stress of the exchange he'd forgotten that. "Sorry. I just get so used to thinking of Hutchins as such a little dollhouse town, I forget people have actual connections and roots here."

The urge to protest that he only thought of it as a dollhouse town because he lived among all those empty McMansions briefly gripped her. But she shook it off—just her own insecurities, trying to derail things. Besides, she remembered her own impression from a few minutes ago, when she'd squatted and put her hand on the lushly watered lawn: the way its verdant healthiness was so clearly too good to be true, the way the cemetery's landscaping seemed somehow to broadcast the cheerful winking dishonesty of a branding campaign. Hadn't she herself always found there to be something fake, hollow, spectral, pasteboard about Hutchins?

Why shouldn't someone hang out at Grandbled? Despite the manicured lawn and so forth, the place was still more anchored in reality than the rest of Hutchins. The death anchored it.

"Sorry about your grandma," Bud said.

"It's okay."

She began walking slowly toward the parking lot. He followed her, uncertainly, weaving a bit as if he might strike out in a different direction, if she signaled she wanted to be rid of him. Clearing her throat, she said, "So, uh. You want to show me the mausoleum with the dog and the sons?"

His face lit up. "You want to see it? You've really never seen it before?"

Hanging out in a graveyard and cruising the markers wasn't so bizarre. Why did she have to be so mean? Well, because she was lonely, and nervous about blowing it if she ever *did* hook up with anybody. Plus she really was self-conscious about being nothing but a loser prole working in a retail chain store, and so when he'd started slipping hints about his income, she'd bristled.

He still looked discombobulated, this painful mixture of shyness and guilt. Presumably the guilt was because he felt he'd offended her earlier, when she'd been, well, acting offended. The ideal fix would be to simply tell him everything she'd just been thinking. Why not? None of her hang-ups were particularly unusual. Talking about them might help break the ice, would help account for her stand-offishness, would give them an interesting subject for conversation (unless Bud laughed at her, in which case she'd know right away he was an asshole and would thus save time).

But she knew she wasn't going to say any of that. It didn't matter how good an idea it was.

While she brooded over her personality flaws, Bud suddenly said, "What is *that*?" She snapped back to the sunny cemetery. Bud continued: "Since when has *that* been here?"

Atop a rise, a tangled mass of vines had sprouted from a grave.

"Are they always so shitty about maintaining the grounds?" she asked, shocked.

Bud shook his head. "That was not there last weekend."

Sally tabled the implication that Bud came to the cemetery every weekend. "You must have missed it," she said. "I don't believe even kudzu could grow like that in just a week."

27

"I would have noticed it."

Bud started climbing up the rise to get a closer look at the overgrown grave.

Sally hesitated. A bad feeling emanated from that grave, she would have said, if she hadn't been too embarrassed to say a thing like that. She pushed herself on up the incline.

Bud stood over the wild, gray-green spray, staring down at it. "Have you ever seen this stuff before? Is it, like, native to Hutchins?"

Sally grimaced. Somehow, she didn't even like looking directly at the spew of vegetation. "I'm not a botanist. But no, I don't guess I've ever seen stuff like this."

"Maybe it's some exotic, introduced species." Bud's tone carried a whiff of environmentalist prudery. "Some kind of plant that was buried with this person, for sentimental reasons." He peered at the tombstone, but the name of the grave's occupant was obscured by the weed. He seemed reluctant to touch the weed, to pull its vines out of the way.

"Coffins are sealed up," she said. "I don't see how a plant could sprout from inside one."

"Maybe someone left some foreign plant on top of the grave, then, in remembrance, and it had seeds that took root."

"Anyway, we should let the groundskeeper know, so he can rip it up."

"Yeah. Totally." He was still staring at it, though. Sally got the impression that, while the sickly-grayish yet robust tangle of vines repulsed Bud, it fascinated him, as well. Fair enough. Nevertheless, despite the bright sunny day and the fact that it was just a plant, her instinct was to get the fuck away from it.

Bud might be interested in the weed. But he also seemed interested in Sally, she couldn't help but be pleased to note. "Yeah, you're right, maybe we can stop by the cemetery's office and see if anybody's there." He started to follow her lead in edging away from the plot.

A rustling sound brought them up short.

Even as she froze and felt her eyes swing toward the vines, she wondered what design flaw in the human brain made that her first reaction. Shouldn't she be moving *away* from the suspicious sound emanating from the creepily violated grave?

Bud froze, too. The nose of something started to emerge from the miniature jungle.

"What is that?" he said, doing a passable job of firming the quaver in his voice.

"I think it's just a mouse," said Sally, keeping her own tone reasonable and calm.

"Yeah, but why is it moving that way...."

Bud was right, there was something unnatural about the smooth motion of the animal's little nose as it slowly but steadily poked its way out from the vegetation. Something off about its eyes, too, and the angle of its neck; and its mouth was open. As it inched out Bud and Sally saw that its front paws were not moving. Right after that the snake emerged, mouth clamped over the mouse's hindquarters.

Sally screamed and reflexively leaped into Bud's arms. He screamed too, and seemed on the verge of pivoting so as to put her body between himself and the snake. But then he must have remembered that he was the man, because he positioned their bodies so as to place himself between her and the reptile.

But when she said, "Kill it, kill it!," his response was, "No fucking way." He and Sally scrambled back down the slope, clinging to each other for protection, keening in fear.

At the bottom of the hill they looked back as if the snake might be pursuing them. But it was a fat, slow-moving thing, its skin a green reminiscent of the vines' color, and moreover its meal slowed it down. For the reason the mouse's motion had seemed so odd was that the mouse itself was not moving. It was, in fact, dead, and in the process of being swallowed by the thick snake that had already worked the mouse's back end through its wide jaws and had apparently decided to come out and sun itself as it finished the task of easing the creature down its throat.

29

Bud and Sally trembled in each other's arms, looking back up the hill at the motionless snake. It loomed outsize in their minds.

Bud got his trembling under control, and gave Sally a reassuring pat on the shoulder. "Wait here," he said, and started back up the hill.

"Stop!" cried Sally.

He didn't stop, but he did say over his shoulder as he climbed, "Don't worry—I don't think it's a poisonous snake—I think it's one of those constrictor types."

Sally would have liked to have known how the hell he knew. She wrung her hands.

She was not the damsel-in-distress type; but she had to admit to finding mildly attractive the notion that Bud was going to do something as manly as march up there and kill that snake. But he gave it a wide berth as he climbed, circling around so as to approach the grave from behind. The snake seemed to be just sunning itself. And, presumably, continuing to work the mouse down its throat.

Bud crept up behind the grave. Sally didn't know how he was planning to kill that thing—the graveyard was too tidily manicured for there to be any sticks lying around on the hill— she supposed he could just stomp on its head, though she wasn't sure she could watch....

He started gingerly tugging the vines away from the tombstone, keeping a nervous eye on the snake. Sally couldn't help imagining all the other monsters that might be hiding in that patch of vines, which, like the snake, had assumed larger-than-life proportions in her head.

"Bud. Bud." The word came out as a wheezy whisper that couldn't possibly have carried all the way up the hill.

He kept pulling back the vines, then looked at the stone. Reading the name on it, she realized. He came back down the hill, again giving the snake a wide berth.

"Amy Madden," he said once he was back. "Ever heard of her?"

Sally stared at him. "Why would I have heard of her?"

He shrugged. "Small town," he said.

They walked together to her car. At first she wondered if that was because he was planning to put the moves on her or otherwise be creepazoid, but no; her car was just on the way to his. He pointed it out, twenty yards further down the path. A late-model Lexus. Nice car, but not hyper-douchy.

She stopped at her own, a fifteen-year-old orange hatchback plastered with sassy bumper stickers. He paused, too. "Well," she said. "This has been a crazy experience."

"Yeah," he said, and wiped his palms on his khaki trousers. "Hey, would you like to hang out sometime?"

Sally burst out laughing.

Wounded, Bud started backing away toward his own car. "Sorry," he said. "I didn't mean to."

"No, no, no!" protested Sally. "*I'm* sorry. I didn't mean it like that. It's just, you know. Of all the times to get asked out. While I'm being chased by a man-eating snake while visiting the grave of my grandma."

"A *mouse*-eating snake," he corrected her. "Anyway, why should we expect there to ever be a better time?"

"True dat." Sally smiled at him. There was something open about the guy. Wholesome, even. He might occasionally put his foot in his mouth, but she got the vibe that if, for example, she were to text him a picture of her boobs (not that she would), he wouldn't share the picture with his office buddies.

"Let me give you my number," she said, and he hurriedly pulled his phone out of his pocket so he could feed it in. His eagerness hovered near the border between cute and desperate, but it was far enough over on the cute side for Sally. Especially after the last few years she'd had, romantically speaking. More like years she hadn't had, considering their uneventfulness. Once he had the number fed in, he called her phone, and she recorded his incoming data.

That ritual completed, she smiled at him and said, "Okay. Well, see you soon, I guess.... What do you want to do, by the way?"

She assumed he would say dinner. Instead, with an utterly innocent face, he said, "Pool party?" Sally blinked. *Um, okay.*

They each went to their cars and left the cemetery, waving at each other as they left. Only after she was gone did Sally realize that, what with all the datey emotions, they'd totally forgotten to drop by the office and complain about the weed snarl, and tell them about the snake.

# Five

Bud felt giddy and imbalanced as he returned home from Grandbled Cemetery, what with the indefinable eerie quality of the strange vines, the adrenal terror of seeing the snake with that mouse macabrely jammed in its jaws, and the joy of getting the cute girl's phone number. He felt ashamed of his level of pride in scoring those digits. If he had been getting it on with women as often as he should then simply getting a phone number wouldn't be a big deal.

Cory was in front of the big plasma TV watching an action movie. When Bud entered the living room Cory's eyes slid his way cautiously. "Hey, dude." They'd only briefly seen each other that morning, and things were still a little weird.

"Hey, cuz," said Bud. He stood with his hands in his pockets, grinning at the TV and nodding appreciatively as if the movie were a new boat Cory had purchased. "Whatcha watchin'?"

"I dunno."

Bud nodded some more, deeply, as if Cory had given an unexpected but wholly satisfying answer, one that would take time to digest. His eyes drifted helplessly to the towel stretched out on the eggshell carpet before the TV. He'd been unable to quite scrub out the stain left by the liquefied shit he'd spilled, and was using the towel to hide the evidence until he could bring more industrial means to bear.

"Hey," he said now, shifting to a deeper, more serious tone. "Listen, man. I want to apologize for last night."

Cory screwed his face up and made a show of trying to figure out what Bud was talking about, before saying, "Oh, *that*? When you were out here, and all? Don't even *worry* about it, bro."

33

"It was wrong of me to subject you to that and I'm sorry."

"Yo dude, your roof your rules."

"I think I might have been in some kind of fugue state, actually."

"Yeah?" Cory dulled his tone and moved his gaze back to the TV, ostentatiously engaging his attention elsewhere.

Probably for the best. "Well," announced Bud. "I'm gonna head up to my room. Gonna take a nap, I think."

"Sounds good, man. Feel better."

Bud went upstairs to his bedroom. In his adult life Bud had never intentionally taken a nap. He'd claimed to want one only because he'd needed an excuse to get away from Cory; the raw shame of having shat and cum in front of his cousin hadn't worn off yet. But once he was in the sanctum of his room he realized that a nap really was what he wanted. So he turned off the light and drew the curtain. Light still seeped through the curtain fabric, and it was funny to be in the blue-tinged room, to be hanging out in the middle of the day in a room with the lights off. He took off his clothes, hung them neatly over his desk chair, and in only his underwear slipped under the bedsheet. Somehow taking a nap felt like an adventure, in its small way. It was an activity he associated with being very young, but also with being very adult, the kind of thing responsible folks who took care of their bodies did.

No need to give himself a medal, though. He closed his eyes and waited, a little curiously, to see if sleep would come.

The muffled sounds of Cory's action movie drifted in through the walls and floor. People screaming, explosions, gunfire, car crashes; but floating in from a distance this way they were kind of peaceful. Bud decided to let the sounds lull him away.

He heard the smothered sound of another explosion. But this one kept going, and going; like it was being stretched out; like the tape was being slowed, except the sound didn't deepen, it only grew longer in duration. Much longer. In fact, its static burble gave no sign of winding down, but stretched on monotonously, till Bud started to wonder if it was even an explosion at all. Resisting the temptation to open his eyes (as if he would somehow be able to see the cause of the sound), he tried to think what else it could be.

It could be something tearing, he supposed. Something thick.

In fact, now that this possibility had occurred to him, Bud no longer was even sure the sound was coming from the downstairs television. It was definitely coming from below him. But now he wondered if it might not be coming from under his bed. Here in the room with him.

The more he listened to that low rumblesome tearing, the less distant it seemed. Not so much muffled, as discreet, secret.

His breath quickened and grew shallow as he realized that it sounded like the floor was being slowly torn open.

A moment ago he'd been relaxing, feeling he might peacefully drift off to sleep. Now his body was clenched, and he kept his eyes squeezed shut not because he was hoping to drift off, but because of the possibility that, if he could keep whatever the threat was from entering his visual field, and therefore from fully entering his mental field, he could keep it from coming into existence.

That ripping rumble continued, but now with another sound on top of it. A kind of slithering, as if whatever was working the chasm open had effected enough of a breach to begin sending at least a part of itself through the gap.

Bud tried to stop breathing, so that his chest wouldn't move and he wouldn't make any noise and the thing might not notice him. But the air pushed and pulled in and out of his lungs in whimpery gasps. Hot sweat covered his body. Somewhere along the line, without really noticing, he had become terrified.

There totally was something present in the room with him. No more was it merely that he could hear the rough soft scrape of its slithering. Now he could feel the oh so subtle shift in the bedsheets, as something touched the mattress with its extremity. Strange odd currents fluttered through the room's energy field as some new presence interacted with it.

Simply keeping his eyes shut was not going to keep the presence from becoming a full-blooded manifestation, he realized with despair. It would only blind him and make him even more helpless. He was going to have to open them.

He did open them.

The whimper sighed out of him. What he saw edging up over the side of the bed, brushing luxuriously against the sheets, was the thick gray-green rope of a vine, or maybe a snake. The snakevine ended in a bulge, almost like a bulb. Except there was a slit in the bulb, a mouth-like slit, a vertical mouth; the inner walls of the slit were a very dark pink, and covered with sprays of white needle teeth. Was it an animal mouth, or something closer to the "mouth" of a Venus flytrap? Was the thing some kind of triffid, or what?

The mouth-like, toothy cavity was also an eye. Bud didn't know what made him think that, but he felt certain it was true—he didn't know how well the thing could see, whether it was like a flatworm eye that could detect only motion and variations of light, but he was sure the opening doubled as this thing's organ of perception.

Forcing himself to breathe more quietly, he began to edge away from the thing toward the opposite side of the bed from where it had sprouted. The thing paused; it hovered upright, the orifice following his progress just like an empty eye; clearly it was aware of him, aware of his motion, and yet even in spite of the impossibility of escaping its notice he continued to scoot himself along with the most agonizing slowness. It wasn't that he had any hope of fooling the snakevine thing. He just wanted it to know that he respected it enough to fear it.

With the thing hanging there in mid-air, grotesque and stately, regarding him, he slowly slid all the way to the other side of the bed, and eased himself off the mattress. The thing continued to watch him. He thought he heard a steady hiss, like air leaking out of a spaceship. But the noise was very soft, and he couldn't be sure that he heard it.

"I can open the window for you," he said, and gave a little nod. He wondered why he'd nodded like that. Then he realized he'd meant it as a bow.

36

There was no use waiting for the snakevine to convey whether it wanted the window open or not—Bud would just have to open it, and pray the action was pleasing to the thing.

He turned, took the curtain, and drew it back. Flame pressed against the window pane from the other side. The flame really did *press*, its solid flickering squishy against the glass. Gelatin flame. Light that it provided poured into the room, yet it didn't hurt Bud's eyes to stare into it. The cold seeping through the window let Bud know how incredibly, hellishly frigid the fire was, too cold for him to dare touch the glass.

He turned around and faced the snakevine again. Bud now he realized it hadn't dug its way up from under the bed, but was a part of him. If he followed with his eyes the gray-green rope down from where its head-like bulge reared up and faced him, all the way down the thing's body, then he saw that actually its body was his own—its yards-long girth spooled out through the cotton of his tighty-whities.

Looking back up at the other end, he saw that he'd been mistaken—it did not end in a bulge with a toothy orifice— instead the snakevine ended in the front half of a rat's body, a phallic sewer centaur. The rat was black and big and stared at Bud with its red eyes as its forepaws clenched. Its chittering sounded like laughter. The whole tentacle swayed back and forth as the rat-head kept eye contact with Bud. The feel of the air sliding along its girth and the undulations of the tentacle felt good to Bud.

Although light did come streaming through the window behind Bud (light warm in color but cold to the skin), it scattered around the room in irrational and dramatic patterns. Large pools of unmotivated black shadows swelled and gaped throughout the room. In one of those jet pools, he realized, was someone.

He couldn't make out her form. He knew it was female not because of any visual cues, but only thanks to a specific sort of tingling in his tentacle.

Maybe there was the barest hint of the sight of something. Maybe some stray gleam reflected off some surface somewhere, and penetrated the well of shadow that had settled in the middle of the room for some reason, in a spot that ought to have been smack in the path of the firelight. Anyway, for whatever reason, Bud felt he could make out what he thought was a ballcap.

The rat-head of his tentacle was penetrating into that shadow, drawing near that ball-capped female form. Bud had no control over it, though he was privy to the ripples of deadly pleasure traveling down its nerves. As it descended into the inky shadow, it became invisible to Bud, so that not only could he not control what the tentacle was doing, he couldn't even see it.

For some reason he glanced down, past the swelling root of the thing tucked into his underwear, all the way down to his bare feet on the carpet. He saw that the fibers of the carpet were mingled with the fibers of his flesh. He himself, he realized, was nothing but threads of flesh and nerves woven together. Not only was he interwoven with the carpet, so that it would have been impossible to lift him off the floor without ripping off his feet or else ripping away part of the floor; he understood that in fact those fibers ran all the way to the female in the shadow. Actually, he was woven from the same stuff as her. He was nothing but an extension of her, a pile of excess stuff that it had pleased her for some reason to fashion into his present form. This relieved him. It implied that she was the one controlling the motion of the tentacle, and so he couldn't be held responsible for it. It made him less nervous about accepting those waves of mysterious pleasure being transmitted along his tentacle from somewhere in the dark. Presumably that pleasure data was being transmitted back along the fibers running through his feet and then the carpet, all the way back to her. Probably she was responsible for exciting them in the first place.

Suddenly, from within that void of shadow, there was a pinching spike of pleasure so sharp it made him gasp. Then he realized with panic that it wasn't pleasure at all, but pain.

When he awoke later, he would have no memory of his dream's details after this point.

# Six

Pretty freaky dream. But whatever. Bud's main focus was on Sally and that pool party. He called her and was relieved and surprised when she agreed, with no fuss, to come over on Monday, tomorrow, after work.

That was awesome, but he couldn't help but worry about her. It wasn't safe to go to strange men's houses that way. *He* knew he wasn't going to rape and murder her, but how could *she* know that? He hoped she was carrying some mace, at least.

He went into FlashComm with a song in his heart, although he tried not to let his coworkers catch on—it would have looked funny....

He and Sally had agreed she would come over at seven, but he left work early anyway so that he could pick up stuff from the supermarket on the way home: a couple twelve-packs of fancy beer, a party platter, assorted chips and dips. Ground beef and hamburger buns so he could finally use that grill he'd bought. Cory had agreed to stay upstairs during Bud's pool party. It was still well before six when Bud got home.

Cory stood in the driveway waiting for him. "You mind if I hang out with you guys tonight?" he asked. "Just for the first little while, is all!" Bud asked him to help carry in the groceries.

Cory was bubbling over with excitement about the upcoming festival. It was annoying listening to him yap about it, and Bud worried that Sally would think he was a loon by association. But it worked out. When Sally showed up, she seemed about as nervous as he felt. If the two of them had been alone, there would have been lots of awkward silences. Cory's enthusiastic touting of the festival's program gave them something to talk about, and it also gave Sally and Bud something to bond over as they explained to blithe, earnest Cory that everything he said was insane. It was fun to argue with Cory, Bud realized, as long as you had someone alongside you, to gang up on him with.

Thank God she turned out to have some basic respect for rationality. How awful, if she'd been on Cory's side and believed in all his mumbo-jumbo.

He had planned to make hamburgers and was humiliated to realize he couldn't figure out how to turn on his new grill. But Sally seemed genuinely not to care that they ordered pizzas instead. She offered to pay for half of them, and Bud declined her offer, managing to be, he thought, chivalrous but not patronizing. The delivery boy got briefly lost in the imposingly empty neighborhood, with all its identical houses, and while they waited for him to arrive Sally changed into her swimsuit (she'd actually brought a swimsuit; Bud had asked her to, but had been afraid she'd find the request creepy and decline). Once the pizzas arrived they took all the food and the cooler full of beers out to the deck. They left plates of pizza and open beer bottles by the edge of the pool, and returned to munch and drink now and then when they weren't floating around. It was perfect.

Especially since Cory didn't spend a lot of time in the water. He splashed around a few minutes, but then hopped out and sat in a deck chair, drinking beer and holding forth.

Right now he was talking about a speaker at the upcoming festival who had developed a perpetual-motion machine. "I'm telling you," he patiently explained for the fourth time, "he's a genius. And what's really inspiring about him is that you never would guess it. He seems like a regular fifty-year-old dude. But he invented this perpetual-motion machine just by tinkering around in his garage like a real, old-fashioned inventor. Now he just needs to get backing, but he can't because nowadays all the money is tied up in corporations, and these corporate backers don't have the vision to see how big a deal this is."

"I think corporations would totally think perpetual motion is a big deal," said Bud. "I mean, basically you're saying that the guy has defeated entropy, right? So you could potentially be talking about, like, an unlimited energy source. Better than cold fusion. Limitless wealth. Untold technological advances. Ecological salvation. Immortality."

Cory nodded, with a sad, sage little smile. "I know," he agreed. "They're shooting themselves in the foot."

Bud was having a blast, because he got to show off to Sally and feel smart by countering Cory's claims. Although he did hope that Cory would go to bed early. It would be nice to have some time alone with Sally at the end of the evening, now that Cory had helped them break the ice.

They'd gotten him wound up, though. Cory turned his attention more exclusively on Sally, since he wanted to talk about Hutchins now and she was a native. Apparently some folks from Hutchins had been relatively big deals, in occult circles. At least, so claimed the festival being held in Hutchins's vicinity. Bud found it hard to believe. Just promo shit, no doubt.

Sally seemed to agree. "I've never heard of any ... uh ... big occult celebrities from around here," she said, with a dubious grimace. With the multicolored dusk above her and surrounded by the sparkling blue water, Bud was astonished by how beautiful she was. He couldn't imagine why he'd thought her an ordinary, borderline-plain girl.

"You should look into them. Like, supposedly there's this one guy who used to be a dowser back in the eighties. And there was a girl. Supposed to be a super-powerful alchemist. Amy Madden."

Both Bud and Sally had drifted into the center of the bowl-shaped pool, where the water was deepest. Now, as their faces snapped to look at each other, they froze and started to sink before they remembered to start treading water again. "Amy Madden?" they both said.

"Yeah," said Cory, looking keenly at Sally, "you've heard of her?" Then he squinted at Bud. "*You've* heard of her?"

Sally started telling Cory about the overgrown grave. Bud winced; Cory was going to latch on to this. He'd been hoping that Cory would soon go away. Now who knew how long he'd yap?

41

Sure enough.... "Dude, her grave was covered in some mysterious plant no one ever heard of before?! And you saw a snake crawling around choking on a rat?! Dudes, that all sounds like some crazy omen."

"It wasn't *choking* on the mouse, it was *eating* the mouse," said Bud. "You believe in omens too? Come on, Cory. You can't just believe in *everything*."

"I go where the universe takes me, bro. I mean, dude, it's *got* to mean something that you guys get exposed to something having to do with Amy Madden, so soon after I learned about her! It's like it's a clue. Like I'm supposed to be here right now."

Bud's and Sally's hands were occasionally brushing as they treaded water, and Bud was starting to strongly feel that Cory *shouldn't* be here, actually. "Don't you think it's just a coincidence, man?"

Cory couldn't stop himself from laughing at Bud's naïveté, before he remembered that it was cruel to scoff at another's ignorance. "Naw, dude," he said. "What are the odds of a convergence like this just being random? Me just happening to be drawn to Hutchins at the same moment a powerful supernatural node like Amy Madden is starting to manifest on this plane through, like, vines and snakes and shit? No way, man.... You know, if she really is using, like, plants and snakes to communicate from beyond the grave, then this could be just the sort of proof of the afterlife that researchers have been looking for for years now."

"Well, what makes her such a powerful node, or whatever?" asked Bud.

"I don't know," said Cory, blinking, uncharacteristically taken aback and unable to conjure an answer. "I just remember reading her name. I *think* in connection to the festival? Must have been. Anyway, I'm sure she was an alchemist."

"Sometimes we don't know till later why the universe has placed us where we are," intoned Sally. Bud's heart flurried in panic, but seeing the half-smile on her face he realized she was only having a goof. The dimming sunlight added a provocative mystery to her face, or maybe it was simply the perfect sort of light by which to see the mystery that was already there.

Cory didn't notice the gentle mocking quality of her tone. "Totally," he agreed, and then, more enthusiastically, "I'll find out all about her. I'll ask around at the conference. And then I'll do, like, research. There's a town library, right? With records or whatever? Did I ask that already? I'll find out all about her and that'll help you guys figure out why you've become, you know, entwined in this whole big thing. And that can be how I earn my keep."

Finally Cory did go upstairs to the guest room. By then Bud and Sally were out of the pool and lounging on deck chairs—it was a warm night and the air felt good on their skin as they sipped their beers. As always Bud had the urge to drink till he was drunk and eat till he was stuffed, but since he was in the presence of a lady he restrained himself. But he did want to get back in the water—his fantasy of having a nice girl over to swim in his pool with him would only be fully realized if his cousin weren't there with them. Happily, Sally proved amenable. From the way she smiled, Bud almost had the feeling she knew how much this little thing meant to him, and instead of savoring the power that gave her she was content simply to provide him satisfaction.

Back in the water, the conversation continued to flow. They even talked about books—or, well, *a* book, *The Hobbit*, one of the few Bud knew very well. It excited him and made him feel smart to talk about a book with this cute girl, who was so much better-read than he. He made some observation about the scene where Bilbo notices the chink in the scales armoring the dragon Smaug's body; it prompted Sally to laugh, and she seemed to think it a very sharp comment. And Bud was inclined to agree with her, which only made it more irritating later on when he was never able to remember what he'd said.

Bud mentioned the frog-eyed lady at Old Petey's, thinking she might be something they could joke about and bond over. But Sally had no idea who he was talking about, had apparently not noticed her.

They went to the middle of the pool to talk, facing each other as they treaded water. Now that Cory was gone, they talked about normal stuff. Their jobs, mainly. Bud explained his dissatisfactions. Sally had many of the same ones, with the added kick that she barely made any money and had no benefits. They weren't touching, but every time one of the underwater currents stirred by her paddling hands and feet rippled across his flesh, Bud felt a shudder of pleasure.

"This is really cool," said Bud.

"What is?" asked Sally. She thought he was referring to his own pool.

Bud was flustered to realize the communication between the two of them was not as crystal-clear as he'd imagined. "Um, I mean, this. This whole thing. Hanging out with you like this, I mean."

"Oh," she said, and smiled. At first Bud took comfort from that smile. But as he looked more closely at it, he began to feel unsettled. Or, at least, less assured.

Not that there was anything dramatically negative going on behind the smile. In fact, unbeknownst to Bud, she was thinking that this *was* pretty cool ... but that thought naturally led her to recall her various entanglements of the last few years (of her whole life since puberty, when you got down to it), and the memory of that smear of banal nastiness that ran through her life was what darkened her mood.

So it had nothing to do with Bud, except in that she was thinking of all those guys who compared negatively to Bud. But Bud couldn't know that was what motivated the darkening; he assumed it was some flaw she'd seen in him, that was a mystery to himself but nevertheless really, truly there. So there was a boundary between them, thanks to this misunderstanding. And to tell the truth it wasn't really even a misunderstanding, because Sally really was looking ahead, unwillingly, to their shared failure: the memory of all those disappointments amounted to a long training course in being disappointed, and to expect this budding relationship to turn out so differently from all her past ones would have fit some people's definition of insanity.

Even so, it was only a passing shadow, and she was basically having a good time. The sunshine of her smile broke apart that brief dark veneer fast enough that Bud could reassure himself, with some credibility, that he'd only imagined it.

"But, so, anyway," he said. "It seems like Hutchins is a more exciting place than I thought."

"Oh, yeah?"

"Yeah. I mean, what with perpetual motion and this Amy Madden person returning from the dead and all."

At the mention of Amy Madden her good mood faltered again, and more seriously. This time she did a better job of covering it up, though. Grinning, she said. "Oh—I thought for a second you meant because you'd met me."

"Oh," said Bud, more softly. "Well ... that, too, yeah. Mainly that."

Sally's grin widened. He could see it fine, though the sun had set.

# Seven

When Bud went to work the next morning, there was another song in his heart and this time he forgot to hide it. Sally hadn't even spent the night—they hadn't even had sex. If they'd had sex, he would have been nervous now, in its aftermath. Instead they'd talked. It had been a long time since Bud had really talked to anyone—that is, talked primarily for the pleasure of communicating, and not as the means to some goal. Actually, he wasn't sure if he'd *ever* talked that way.

He didn't even gnaw over whether Sally had had as good a time. He was certain she'd felt the same way. That's how intimate the evening had been.

At the coffee machine he dumped extra sugar and powdered cream into his styrofoam cup of coffee, and grinned at the approaching Jason Sterne. "Back at the ol' cubicle farm, hey?" said Bud, more cheerfully and heartily than one normally said things here at FlashComm.

Jason Sterne paused, chin tucked in warily as he eyed Bud with suspicion, not so much as if he thought Bud was putting him on, more as if he feared Bud might go nuts and start shooting people. Once he realized that Bud's unwarranted good humor was not a sign of dangerous imbalance, but merely some sort of oblivious, goofy mood, a superior smile flickered onto his mouth. "Yeah," he said, in a mild, noncommittal voice. He stopped while still a good distance from Bud, so that he had to stretch his arm as far as it would go to reach the styrofoam cups.

Bud dropped his eyes, ashamed of having exposed himself, like a kid that didn't know better. "Okay, well, see ya!" he chirped as he scurried to his cubicle, aghast at his own carelessness;

if he didn't shield this glow in his breast, then it would be extinguished. It was precious, and he ought to be careful with it. Hide it. Happiness makes you ridiculous. Letting himself see his happiness's ridiculousness reflected in the gazes of others would eventually kill it.

Till now he'd never noticed any contempt for him on Jason's part. Even now it didn't occur to him that the contempt and distaste he'd seen had been directed at *him*, particularly—he assumed it had been deployed against Bud's clownishly vivid emotion. But actually, Jason Sterne didn't like Bud. He himself assumed he didn't like Bud because of a general vibe he got off the guy. But the real incitation to his dislike had come shortly after Bud had moved to Hutchins and started at FlashComm. Jason had been sitting outside on the office's deck during his lunch break, moping, dwelling on his wasted life, feeling like an animated trash bag stuffed with ashes. Growing up he had played the clarinet, all through school, even hanging onto the skill until the end of college. Even now, in his shameful secret daydreams, he imagined himself playing in an orchestra, like for a living. Or, more excitingly because it was technically more possible, he imagined himself leaving Hutchins and moving someplace where he could at least find an amateur group to play with. On this particular day Jason had been sitting at the picnic table, his daydreams leaking out of him, chilly in the cold sun, and had seen Bud for the first time as he came out onto the deck. He'd been carrying a bottle of Coke, and a straw in its wrapper. Jason wondered why anyone would use a straw to drink their Coke out of a bottle. Bud paused at the doorway and, instead of peeling the paper wrapper from the straw, he held it in his fist and banged one end of it against the brick wall, using the pressure of the wall to push its other end through the paper. He stuck the tip of his tongue out as he did it, letting it curl up out of the left corner of his mouth like a cartoon character making an effort. The sight of the red straw poking out of the white wrapper made Jason think of a dog getting an erection. It seemed to him that he had never seen anyone

48

do anything stupider-looking in his whole life. If he had really noticed his own reaction, maybe he would have subjected it to some scrutiny, and maybe the impression would have dissolved. Instead it had taken root: Jason Sterne's new co-worker was a vulgar buffoon.

Bud peeked out from his cubicle at Jason going by. Without really noticing, just in these last few minutes, he'd started to think of Jason as his enemy. He logged on to his computer and got to work.

Soon he was navigating snarls of code. The spectre of ridicule at the hands of Jason Sterne receded. So did the warm feeling left over from last night; it receded even further, in fact, being irrelevant to the current environment and the task at hand.

Dimly he became aware that work was sliding by at a nice clip. He was in the zone, as he so rarely was. He let himself sink further into it, relishing his own productivity, the luxurious expanse of time that would be opened up if he could get ahead of schedule.

The pleasure of accomplishment became sharper and sharper, till he was tingling. Now he started to become aware of a certain distance growing in the universe, as the space between atoms grew larger. Sounds became attenuated as the stuff of the world became thinner, allowing them less material through which to vibrate. Bud realized (from too far away to get very excited about it) that this was the prelude to another episode. Like the snakevine, or the dream of the vagina magnet. Instead of getting scared, or being worried that he'd have some sort of collapse here at work and shit himself or something, Bud got excited, in anticipation of the pleasure-pain that had accompanied the last two visions.

Whatever was going to happen, though, he probably did not want it to go down here at the cubicle. He had just enough wherewithal left to lock his computer before hurrying to the men's room, hunching over to hide his hard-on.

Nobody occupied the toilet stalls, thank God. And thank God there was nobody in the bathroom at all, because he slammed through the door like he was fleeing something, clambered into a toilet stall like it was a lifeboat. He giggled at himself as he latched the door. Dropped his pants, sat on the pot. What was even up with him, he wondered? It wasn't like he had to take a shit. Wasn't like he was horny, not exactly, although he did have this hard-on. But it was like he had it by proxy, like the hard-on was there to service some else's excitement; Bud waited obediently for instructions in its use to be transmitted in from somewhere. The cold of the ceramic bowl oozed up through his thighs, webbing through the fatty fibers of his flesh. Skimming along his guts before extending out along his cock, tingling out, radiating crisp coolness from the glans. The whole room grew cool, till Bud could see his foggy breath. Hardly did he notice when the bathroom door whacked open again, when some other body scrambled into the stall beside his, collapsed onto the toilet there. The cold was not harsh, not bitter, the cold was silky, the air like refrigerated satin, gliding its currents along his quivering nude flesh. The fog of breath grew thicker, whiter, more cottony. It was no longer merely his breath; someone was breathing along with him; someone bigger than him was breathing for him, on his behalf. For never could he have created so much breath. He was sitting on frozen air in a cloudy white tube of breath, cold, lust, he suddenly realized, with a rough, building friction as the moist cool envelope moved up and down, up and down, as if he were floating within a soft piston. As the tube in which he hung suspended moved up and down, up and down, the frozen air beneath him banged up into his backside, again and again, a hard slapping rhythm. And he must have new nerves back there, for the repetitive slapping pressure against his buttocks sent waves of exotic pleasure rippling out through the ends of his limbs and up out of the crown of his head. And from eyes whose location would have confused him if he'd thought to ask where they were he saw, far below him, Jason Sterne, greased with blood-clotted slime tasting of maple syrup, being jerkily extruded again and again from the white-fog tube by the slapping action of Bud's frozen-air seat, like a raw babe being banished from the birth canal. Echoing in from the distance came the excited yipping of some huge dog.

Meanwhile, not too far away (in fact as she'd left her car she'd smiled at the FlashComm building), Sally had just entered the mall. On her way to work, but she felt like goofing off a little first. Last night had put her, too, in a good mood, a state of flighty happiness in which she couldn't really concentrate on any of her books. She'd tried watching TV, but had gotten the sense that all the programs were trying to depress her. So she decided upon a little physical activity. She never really took walks, exactly—it would have felt vaguely pretentious, in Hutchins. Sometimes she went to Boonesville Park. But she felt too much wriggly energy for her to be content with nature-gazing.

With Boonesville out, the most obvious way to kill time was to go window-shopping at the mall. As long as she didn't set foot in the Barnes and Noble, it wouldn't feel too much like she was just hanging out at work during her off-hours.

The mall was a two-story glass-and-metal artifact, tubular white struts arranged in dramatic angles holding the glass walls in place. Over the years the white had gotten scuffed. Sally remembered being a little girl, before the mall had opened, riding past in the backseat of her parents' car and seeing it under construction. But she couldn't remember what had been on this spot before the mall. She was always surprised at the number of people milling about—although she always saw folks she knew, she was always surprised to find there were folks she didn't. It seemed incongruous that Hutchins had this many people available. With so many unknown faces, she would have expected unexpected things to happen more often.

As she walked in, disappointment in herself dampened her mood. She should have made the effort to think of something cooler to do with her time. Expending energy by walking around the mall was all right, but gazing at its cavernous, banal interior, she acknowledged that this place held no surprises for her. She should be seeking out new, interesting experiences. Hell, even that goofball Cory had been able to find a speck of this corner of the world that was at least *interesting*; that upcoming fraud-buffet of a conference over in wherever-it-was might not be an intellectual supernova, but as someone who hung out at a mall she had no right to sneer. And there must be still more interesting nooks of Hutchins that she could find, if only she made an effort. Not for the first time, she resolved to quit wasting her life, or at least to waste it a little less, or at the very very least to waste it differently.

Her eyes flickered over the shops: Gadzooks, the Gap, the Banana Republic. A shop called Morgan's with pretentions to being up-scale. She looked at the shuffling shoppers. Most of them weren't even smiling, not even fake smiles. Something heavy began to weigh down on her.

But up ahead on her left were puppies gamboling in a shop window. The pet store! Always she avoided it, because she had no desire to buy a pet. But right now she wasn't here for any utilitarian reason. And the animals, at least, would not be subject to the same creepy zombification as the shoppers. She went to the window and looked at the puppies. Beside her were two teenyboppers, going "ooo" and "aw," slapping hands over giggling mouths and hopping in place each time a puppy flipped onto its back. Sally found their adoration rote and performative, and exactly the sort of thing she'd been trying to avoid in coming to look at the animals. To get away from the humans, she sidled into the pet store.

Here were humans, too, but at least they were going about the legitimate business of buying pet food and leashes and whatnot, meaning they had less of a need to assert their existence with the same sort of noisy prattle as the two teenyboppers. Still, Sally realized that what she really needed was to be away from people altogether, to go elsewhere and nurture this feeling she had inside her. Like a young green shoot, she thought, then winced at the cheesy cliché. These kinds of clichés, and the self-disgusted wincing that accompanied them, were exactly the sorts of things she needed to be protecting the fucking young green shoot from.

She moved further away from creatures like the puppies, and the people that surrounded them. Went towards the back, towards the fish. Less people hung around gawking at the fish. A few, admittedly, in front of the rock stars, like the piranhas. But when Sally turned the corner, she found tanks set up along the back wall teeming with small fish, colorful but otherwise unremarkable. No other shoppers here. She settled in to watch a tank of yellow fish with blue speckles, curious what the experiment's results would be, whether looking at animals frolic, even here inside the mall, would have the same soothing effect as being out in legit nature.

A guy's head popped into existence in the fish tank in front her. His head plunged down into the tank, crown first, eyes and mouth wide. The head was disembodied, but very much alive, like the skin of the water of the tank was an interdimensional portal through which it had been plunged, and its body was still back at the head's point of origin, somehow still pumping blood to its brain even across that undone seam in the cosmos. Not that Sally thought all that out. She just registered, without trying to explain it, that the head was pumping up and down into the tank like a vicious plunger, with no upside-down body attached to disturb the tanks stacked above it. It moved too fast to make out many details of its expression, but the expression wasn't subtle enough for her to need details: eyes bulged and mouth gaped in horror; some of the bubbles suddenly filling the tank were thanks to the churning of the head, but some came from the air being expelled from absent lungs in a shriek of horror. A shriek that was almost, but not quite silent; Sally could hear it, but muffled, by much more than the glass pane and a few inches of water—as if it were dopplering in via some continuum from far, far away. Panicked fish rocked through the violent water. The head must have gulped a lungful of water as the emptied lungs to which it was attached tried reflexively to replenish themselves—Sally was sure she saw a fish get swept helplessly into that gaping mouth and up its throat. Then the head was gone, with a plopping sound as water rushed in to fill the gap its disappearance left. It had probably been there less than four seconds. By the time Sally looked around to see if anyone else had noticed (but no one was around), the water had nearly stopped sloshing. Only the water glistening down the tank and puddling on the floor, displaced by the head's appearance, gave evidence that it had been there at all. Sally edged along the aisle, not wanting anyone to notice her proximity to the spilled water and think she'd been messing with the tanks or the water or the fish. She thought about mentioning the disembodied head to someone. But what would the pet-store people do about it? Also, they'd never believe her. Which was as it should be, because she didn't believe it had happened, herself. She double-checked to be sure: no, she did not believe a living disembodied head had traversed dimensions in order to be dunked in that fish tank. She had perceived it, sure, but nevertheless she absolutely did not believe it. She couldn't. Pausing to look at the bunnies (for form's sake), she left the pet store and walked to Barnes and Noble. She actually thought about going home sick, a thing she never did, but opted against it. For one thing, she couldn't afford to. Besides, there wouldn't be any point. She'd still be just as freaked out by the churning head, whether she was at work or not.

# Eight

When Sally saw the head magically appear and churn the fish tank water, the prospect of a supernatural intervention in her life frightened her. By the time she slipped out of the pet store, what frightened her was the possibility she might be going crazy. But she got through her shift without any more exotic happenings, and with all the usual annoyances of work to distract her. By the time she clocked out, she actually had to stop and ask herself why she was in such a jangly mood, before remembering she'd had a hallucination.

She drove to Bud's. With happy naïeveté, they'd made plans at the end of last night's date to do the exact same thing this evening, as well. A bit of anxiety had niggled its way into her head, but when she double-checked her state of mind she was pleased to find that she still felt basically comfortable going over to Bud's. Usually it took very little for her to regret any emotional access she gave a guy. Probably because most guys she'd gone with had been clumsily manipulative shitheads. Not entirely her fault—pickings in Hutchins were slim. But with Bud she felt a comfortable mix of a warm, moderate sexual attraction and a brotherly vibe. That family vibe was reinforced when Cory came to the door to let her in; "Bud's in the bathroom," he explained nonchalantly.

As she entered she heard a toilet flush; she listened, and was pleased to hear the sound of water running in a sink. So Bud was a guy who washed his hands after using the bathroom—nice. He joined them in the living room, running his fingers through his hair to fix it, saying, "Hey!," a defenselessly glad expression on his face. He embraced Sally. "Sorry," he added, with a jerk of the head back the way he'd come.

As far as Sally could tell, he was apologizing for having been in the bathroom. "Don't worry about it."

They sat on the living room sofa and made small talk while Cory fixed himself a sandwich in the kitchen, then blithely joined them. (Bud had finally gotten the poop stain out of the carpet—now *that* had taken a lot of work!) Cory took a huge bite, nodded at the big-screen TV, and spoke around the food in his mouth: "Dude, it's not healthy to have such a big TV like that right in the middle of the room like that."

"It's not even on," said Bud.

"Doesn't matter. It's still there, present. Like, anchoring the room and the whole household to the state-media complex. Like, it's this massive centralizing element. The trick is to *de*centralize. That's how you humanize stuff. Like, a big TV like that should be hidden away in some other room way off somewhere in the house. Like, in the main living room there shouldn't be a TV at all, or else maybe just like a little one, like a little tiny miniature black-and-white set, over in a corner where it doesn't really attract attention."

"How was your day?" said Bud to Sally.

"Oh, you know. Work was work. Before that I just fiddled around. Stopped by the pet store." After that, her mouth muscles just moved vaguely, not knowing what words to form. She had to mention the pet store, because the freaky occurrence there was the only interesting thing that had happened today. But she couldn't go ahead and explain *what* had happened, because it was nuts.

"Are you getting a pet?" asked Bud.

"No," she said, with an awkward smile. Not mentioning the hallucination had turned the pet-store into a conversational cul-de-sac, and she couldn't figure a way out of it. *So much for the natural rapport,* she said to herself regretfully, then felt that regret sharpen into anger. She could at least try, for fuck's sake!

Bud noticed her awkwardness, and she saw a shadow flit across his face; he was assuming he'd done something wrong. To get them away from whatever his gaffe had been, he changed the subject: "Guy puked at work today and a fish came out."

The sandwich halted on its way to Cory's mouth. "Came out of what?"

"Sorry. Came out of his mouth, I mean."

Cory and Sally both seemed interested, especially Sally, so Bud went ahead with the tale, pleased with himself. He'd debated whether to mention the incident; it was a story about puking, after all, and he didn't want Sally to think of him as a vulgar person. However, it was far and away the most interesting thing that had happened at work today (except for the orgasmic psychedelia in the toilet stall, but he barely remembered that right now, as if his brain was dialed to a setting that had difficulty thinking such thoughts, remembering such experiences). He told them how he'd come across Jason Sterne, leaning against the wall, pale, head inexplicably soaked, gulping down air. (He didn't mention that he'd come across Jason as he himself was leaving the men's room; didn't mention the strange sense of culpability he'd felt upon realizing that Jason had come staggering out of the men's room just before he himself had left it; didn't mention how he'd hung back, he and those office-mates who'd also noticed Jason's apparent illness, all eyeing each other uncertainly, everyone waiting to be sure this actually was a big deal before doing anything.) Jason's raised arm propped him up upon the gray wall, the rest of his body hanging loose, as if a shackle on his wrist bound him and held him upright. A convulsion had passed through his body and rippled across his clammy face; he'd lurched over at the waist and with one emphatic spurt had vomited a jet of clear bile. No food, no chunky stuff—except, that is, for one small fish. A fish that had still been alive, or at any rate fresh enough that it had flopped a while on the light-beige carpet.

"Dude." Cory was awed. "Is there an aquarium at your office?"

"Nope."

"Are you sure?" Sally seemed beyond intrigued—she seemed spooked. "Like, maybe on another floor? Or in some exec's private office?"

"No." Technically, Bud supposed it was possible. But he could not imagine the presence of any vibrant animal life in that office building.

His audience's interest gratified him. Yet at the same time it created an unwelcome pressure. He could feel their desire to know more about this mysterious fish. But that desire clarified to him the fact that, actually, he didn't want to go too deeply into this subject. Because there were things he didn't want to reveal, things he hadn't even been aware of till he'd found himself recounting the event. Like how, watching Jason Sterne's suffering, Bud had remembered the guy's superiority that morning by the coffee machine, and how the sight of his illness and then the humiliation of his public vomiting, and the monstrous secret he'd disgorged, had filled Bud with smug pleasure, a pleasure that made him feel ashamed, now that he remembered it in Sally's presence.

Cory leaned forward, elbows propped on his knees, hungry for details. "You say the fish was still alive? Still flopping around? Even though there were no fish available in the building, meaning it had to have been a long time since he'd eaten it? Dude, that would seem to strongly suggest a supernatural event."

Bud squirmed. "All right, well, I don't know." Shit, he shouldn't have said anything. It wasn't like he could offer any alternative, rational explanation. Yet the topic of supernatural shit stirred vague, unwanted, dreamlike memories.

Cory's eyes bugged. "Well what else could it have been?!"

Sally cleared her throat. "It actually kind of reminds me of something I saw today." And with a nervous laugh, she told her own story, of what she'd seen at the pet store. When it was over, she finished with, "Well, anyway," and a vague, dismissive wave of her fingers.

Bud was giving her the side-eye. Even Cory was speechless. Not for long, though: "Guys, there is totally some sort of connection here!"

58

"Oh, come on, Cory," groaned Bud. "It's only a coincidence."

"*Coincidence?!* She saw a head manifest and swallow a fish, and at about the same time you saw a guy spit the same fish back up! I'll bet you a million bucks it was the same head and the same fish. You guys are in tune to some sort of phenomenon here in town—something's put you on the same wavelength. Did you two have sex last night?"

"Cory. Seriously. Quit."

Sally's arms had crept up to cross over her chest, hugging herself protectively—she noticed, and forced them back down to her sides. She still wanted to be here, wanted to be with Bud, wanted to keep seeing him, liked him. But that fresh safe feeling she'd had about him had dissolved. With these bizarre incidents, their relationship had suddenly become even more fraught than all her prior, generally hideous ones.

Although she didn't really believe in the supernatural, either, she found Bud's refusal to consider it stressful. After all, her vision or hallucination or whatever it had been did seem to line up pretty strangely with his story. "But, Bud, it's fun to talk about anyway," she ventured, in a voice that utterly failed to convey an impression of fun.

He winced, and shot her a look that was almost a glare. "Let's not encourage him. You get to go home, but I have to stay and listen to him."

She couldn't figure out why he seemed so pissed off just to be talking about this stuff. Oh, wait—it must be because he didn't believe her—he thought she was making all this up, as a way to attract attention, or to one-up him, or in a pathetic attempt to make it seem like they had a closer connection than they actually did. She felt wounded and mournful. And offended. All day, she'd been assuming that the churning head had been a wild figment of her imagination; now she wanted to protest that, after all, *something* had happened to her.

She said, "It is *kind* of a weird coincidence, though, you have to admit."

In her look and tone Bud seemed to hear a warning. "Sure," he said. "But that's still all it is. The brain does weird stuff all the time. It just so happens that both our brains did something weird on the same day, that's all."

"But it's not *just* the brain, right? I mean, other people saw this fish that your workmate threw up, right?"

Bud was too savvy to suggest that her churning head had been a mere neural hiccup, while asserting the physical reality of his barfed fish. "Well, I don't know," he said, adopting a reasonable tone. "I'd just assumed they did. But maybe I was the only one who saw it—I'd have to ask the folks at work if they saw it, too."

Cory stared at Bud in bemusement. "You say that like you're trying to normalize stuff, but that would just make it even *more* weird. It's one thing if both of you observed some kind of physical event that's like actually going on. But now you're talking about having some sort of shared vision. Which would mean both of you observed some kind of *psychic* event. Which, okay, I'm down with that too."

Bud shrugged.

Sally felt she should drop it. Not because she was scared to stare down into the abyss of the shadow world. She just didn't want to let a bunch of paranormal garbage screw up her chance to have a nice boyfriend. But she couldn't stop herself from saying, timidly, "My fish was yellow with little blue specks. The fish I saw the head swallow, I mean. Was your fish like that?"

Bud didn't answer. Just sat there like a lump. Stared into space like he'd been beaten at something. His silence gave her all the answer she needed—yeah, yellow with blue speckles. His defeated feeling was contagious, and she wished she hadn't asked the question. But why? Couldn't you even make the case that there was something romantic about their sharing a connection up on the spiritual plane?

Cory said, "It's especially interesting that this would happen right before the festival. Like, there's some connection."

"Maybe something to do with that Amy Madden person." Sally couldn't quite figure out the right tone to use for that suggestion. Not committed—but not merely playful, either.

"Just because, you brought her up the other day. And Bud and I saw that big viney weed on her grave."

Cory nodded sagely. "Exactly. *Exactly*. We should research her."

"*No,*" said Bud, with a vehemence Sally almost found annoying.

But she supposed she ought to at least sort of support him. To Cory, she said, "Yeah, I mean, how would we even do that, anyway? How do you research some random person?"

"Um. The library?"

Well, okay. But she still couldn't quite picture how that would work. You couldn't just walk up to the librarian and be like, "Tell me about Amy Madden." And yet she knew it was possible to research people. In movies, in detective novels, folks were always finding out the most amazing stuff about other people, just by digging around. Suddenly the prospect of performing such a feat, herself, gave her a thrill. Honestly, it almost seemed more exciting to crack the mystery of how the regular world guarded its mundane secrets, than it did to find out what amazing but probably never to be repeated cosmic burp had caused her to see a disembodied churning head swallow a fish at around the same time that Bud had seen a guy barf one up. Almost apologetically, she turned to Bud: "It might be kinda fun, just to see what we can find out."

She'd adopted the apologetic tone mainly as a matter of form. She hadn't expected him to really be offended. Yet he recoiled and shot her a betrayed look. "Come *on!*"

Sally blinked. "I just mean, for the fun of looking. Not even necessarily for the sake of finding out any mysterious connection between this Amy Madden person and any of the stuff we've happened to see. Just, as a thing to do. A thing to do in Hutchins. This place can be such a wasteland sometimes, like it's just floating adrift in time and space. With no history. So I think it would be kind of neat to pick this one person and dig around and see what we learn about her. It might sort of make the town come alive, a little."

"Yeah, but according to that logic it doesn't need to be Amy Madden at all. You could just pick any person at random and investigate them, instead."

Sally shrugged, helplessly. That would be cheating. "Well, but why *not* Amy Madden?"

Bud wouldn't look directly at anyone. "You guys can do whatever." He sounded bitter, like she'd dumped him. "But I'm not into all the voodoo stuff. And if I want to learn about history, I'll brush up on *real* history. Like, I've always meant to read up on the Civil War, but I've never gotten around to it. If I'm going to make the effort to learn about history, I think it ought to be some sort of history like *that*. Not the history of some random dead girl in Hutchins."

"Well. Sure." Now Sally felt offended, and wasn't exactly sure why. She dug around inside herself to try to figure it out; startled, she realized she took issue with his apparent contempt for Hutchins. "I mean, obviously, if something doesn't interest you, you shouldn't worry about it."

Now he looked at her, with a grimace that told her he knew he'd screwed up, and would have liked to apologize, but couldn't articulate what he'd done wrong well enough to do so.

Cory gave no sign that he noticed anything untoward. He clapped his hands and rubbed them together. "Awesome! I'll start googling her tonight!"

Sally and Bud were still looking at each other, with that regretful, resigned feeling. Neither of them could see how to extricate themselves from this quicksand they'd wandered into, but Sally could sense that at least they were both willing to wait it out. "You want a beer?" he asked her, as a peace offering.

"Sure. Thanks. Are they just in the fridge? I can go get them."

"No, no, no, I'll go," he said, and hurried up off the couch and out of the room.

# Nine

Sally didn't stay the night at Bud's. She'd been asking herself when she would start sleeping with him—she was generally a second-or-third-date kinda gal, but the presence of his houseguest complicated things. And what with the discordant vibe that had sprung up between them, Sally felt glad that Cory was there. If they'd been alone and he'd made a pass and she'd declined, it would have been awkward; he might have thought she was rejecting him on account of Amy Madden. Having Cory around made the question moot.

On the other hand, if they'd been alone they could have changed the subject. But Cory prattled on and on about Amy Madden, and about her possible but increasingly improbable connection to every scrap of alleged weirdness mentioned in the program of his upcoming festival. He kept returning to alchemy. Sally couldn't see what connection alchemy had to either the overgrown grave, or the mouse-eating snake, or the churning head and barfed fish.

She might have become interested in the possibility of a link if Bud had mentioned his dream of the apothecary. But he kept that to himself. Kinda didn't even remember it, exactly.

The next day, Wednesday, she was off until the evening shift. She and Bud made plans for Friday after work (she had the day shift Friday). They did so a little warily, both of them aware that a new element had entered their relations.

On the way to the library she made two wrong turns, and had to take an extra-long pause at a stop sign to examine her mental map of Hutchins. Embarrassing; if it hadn't been so many years since she'd visited the library, she would have had the route at her fingertips.

Of course, she had commenced her research with her phone, by googling "Amy Madden." And lo and behold, she'd gotten a hit: an obituary, from 1997. Amy Madden had been struck by a car and killed, here in Hutchins.

The obituary was the only reference to an Amy Madden in Hutchins that Sally was able to find online. Perversely, she felt grateful for that. If there'd been a wealth of material available on the internet, she would have been stuck at her apartment all day, on the computer. Part of the attraction of investigating all this shit was getting out of her rut, physically. Going to the library, doing a little legwork. Hitting the books.

That did leave the question of which books to hit, and just how to hit them. She walked into the library, then stopped short. Now what? The tan-and-beige interior was sparsely populated: a couple of teenagers hunched over a table in the Graphic Novels section, giggling and squawking over the comics piled up on their table; a chubby mom with her three toddlers, all braying at each other. At the front desk a thirty-something redhead, the librarian, glanced up at Sally, smiled tightly, then returned to whatever she was reading. Hoping to be left alone till the time came for her to clock out. Sally could relate.

Sally might not have been in a library for years, but she had at one point daydreamed about becoming a librarian. After all, she liked books, and it seemed like a generally non-sucky job. But then she'd found out you needed a whole degree in something called Library Sciences. That put paid to that.

She drifted a few more steps into the library, trying to look contemplative instead of simply lost. She loved books—why didn't she come here more often? Or, like, ever? Why should the library be such an alien environment? Well, she supposed it was because what she really loved was *buying* books, more than reading them…. That wasn't fair, but it was true that in her apartment she had piles of books that she couldn't really afford, even with an employee discount, and that were mostly aspirational—she'd never get around to half of them, and probably a quarter of them were intellectually hefty tomes, too dense for her. But at least they were there, real, solid. Whereas getting books from the library felt so transient, so dream-like and unsubstantial. Even if you read them all, once you gave them back weren't you left with nothing?

Sliding her eyes across the interior she saw with a jolt that Cory was here, too. Sitting at a table with his back to her, leaning over a book, but she recognized the back of his head. Seeing him kicked her into gear; she didn't particularly want to collaborate with him on this—his scatterbrained zaniness would drag her down—so she had better get situated and tucked away somewhere before he noticed her. She advanced to the front desk. The librarian smiled warmly with her mouth while her eyes begged to be left in peace. Sally tried to reassure the librarian with the gentlest, most undemanding smile she could muster. In a soft tone, almost whispering, as if she were in an old-fashioned quiet library from a movie, she said, "Hi, I was wondering if you could help me with the microfiche?"

The librarian's widening smile couldn't conceal her dismay. "Microfiche?" she repeated, at a normal speaking volume.

"Or microfilm. I don't really know the difference. What I want is to look at local newspapers from 1997."

The librarian got up and led Sally back to the microfilm-viewing station at the back of the building. (Turned out microfilm was what the library had—not microfiche.) At first Sally couldn't diagnose the tension bunching the librarian's shoulders. Then, once it came to locating the desired newspaper records and unspooling them into the reader, she realized it was the forced bravery of a woman marching to her doom. The librarian had no clue how to operate this stuff. No doubt she'd once been trained in it, but in all the years the woman had been working at the library, this was probably the first time anyone had requested help with microfilm. The woman was trying valiantly to recall her training, but to no avail. Sally watched her flailing, and guiltily tried to think of how to give her some reprieve before her incompetence became unignorable.

"Hey, yo, Sally, what's up?"

At first Sally was annoyed to see Cory appear at her elbow. But then he turned out to be an old hand at microfilm. As he found the Hutchins Gazette for the months surrounding Amy Madden's death and inserted them into the reader, the librarian watched, hoping to give the impression that she was gently supervising the precocious visitor, while in fact trying to memorize the process for the unlikely event that she would ever again need the knowledge. Once the reader was all set up she retreated back to the front desk and her book.

Cory showed her the book he'd been reading (Sally was grateful for the distraction, since now that the microfilm was inserted she wasn't sure what came next—was she supposed to just read every issue of the newspaper from 1997?). It was the yearbook from 1995, Amy Madden's tenth-grade year. A pretty smart place to start, Sally had to admit. Her displeasure at being outdone by a guy who believed in garage tinkerers inventing perpetual-motion machines made her feel petty.

"Check this out," he said, opening the book. "I went through every page of this thing, and there's only two pictures of Amy Madden. If you can call them that." He flipped to them both and showed Sally. There was her portrait, placed in alphabetical order along with all the other tenth-graders. And in the back of the book, among the allegedly candid photos of student life—kids mugging for the camera, or caught in moments of quiet if unconvincing contemplation—there was a shot of her sitting on the grassy swell alongside the library wall (Sally had gone to Hutchins High a few years later, and recognized the landmark). In both of them she wore a ball cap, which was strange for the yearbook portrait. Stranger still, her face was obscured. The black-and-white image bubbled and blurred between her neck and ball cap, in both photographs.

Sally frowned, a little creeped out. She ran her fingers along the glossy paper, to see if the book had been vandalized. As far as she could tell the image had been printed this way. One marred photo might have been a mistake, albeit a suspiciously specific mistake considering that it obscured only the face. But blotting out both instances of her face clearly was on purpose. "I guess someone on the yearbook committee didn't like Amy Madden," she hazarded.

"Yeah," said Cory, almost in a grunt. He sounded like he had reservations.

"You don't think so?"

"*I* don't know. Only, let's not assume right off the bat it was intentional."

Sally didn't see how it could have been anything else. But she remained impressed enough by Cory's microfilm prowess to give his pathological open-mindedness a pass. "Maybe there are better pictures of her in the '96 or '97 yearbook."

"Nah, she's not in them. Not in the yearbooks for the other two high schools, either, I checked. I bet you she dropped out."

Sally looked again at the photo of Amy Madden sitting by the library, studying everything that had been left unobscured. Her fraying denim cut-offs, her black metal-band T-shirt, her ballcap. Her skinny legs and skinned, knobby knees, her filled-out chest. All pretty normal—and yet Sally shuddered, and thought, *I bet you're right.*

Cory said, "Anyway, that's all I found so far. Her face being blurred out is pretty weird. But the most interesting stuff is still just that obituary that's online. The stuff about how she died."

Sally frowned. "What, just that she got hit by a car? You think there was something suspicious about that?"

Cory grinned. "Oh, you didn't figure all that out about the address? That road the obituary says she got hit on, I googled it and it's the old name of the street Bud lives on. Dude, I bet you she got killed right in front of his front door."

# Ten

The previous three visions, Bud could sort of remember, if he made the effort. Not in great detail, and always with the bulk of the sensation packed away in some sealed crevice of his body, leaving the memories colorless and numb. This time, though, he couldn't remember at all what had happened. Only snatches of images and impressions remained to flit and tease past his mind's eye: skin of a crimsoning sheen, scabby knees and perfect tits, an old moist ball cap that stank of sweat and sperm. Also the impression of a deep scarlet venomous pleasure that had soaked into his flesh. He felt a smug, proud satisfaction even with the hollow brittle simulacrum that had been left him in the place of true sensation. If he'd been able to recall it, the mere memory of whatever she'd done would have overpowered him. It never would have occurred to him to share the experience with a friend, even if he'd still had access to it himself.

When Cory and Sally showed up he was sitting in his armchair in the living room before the cool fireplace, broodingly savoring this latest visitation, mind too blank to even know he was thinking about it. At the sound of the doorbell he roused himself, made himself normal, gave Sally a hug and a peck on the cheek and said "Hey dude" to Cory.

He might even have felt normal by the time they reached the living room, the strange vision might have faded, like a childhood trauma that may be present but that you never fully remember. But Sally and Cory were prodding the subject awake even before they got to the couch, both of them bubbling over and raring to talk about Amy Madden.

"She died *right here*, dude," Cory kept saying. "Like, right at your front door!"

"We don't actually know that, for sure." Try as she might to be responsible and keep her enthusiasm in check, excited awe crept into Sally's words. "The obituary doesn't say in front of which lot the car accident happened, it just says it was on this street. Or, I mean, on the street this used to be, back before they renamed it and built this development. Back then, there weren't any houses out here. I guess the lots weren't even numbered, or the land wasn't even divided into lots, so they couldn't have been more specific even if they'd wanted to."

"But they are, like, *very* unspecific, dude," said Cory. "Like, we backtracked from the obituary and found the newspaper story about the hit-and-run. And there's, like, *no* details. And I couldn't find any follow-up stories over the next couple weeks, none of the usual community-outrage bullshit. I bet anyone who knew Amy Madden was glad to know she was gone, that's the subtext I get."

Bud's mouth twisted into a dubious grimace. "Pretty big jump, there."

"Intuition, dude! I'm telling you, she was a bug up the ass of the good folks of Hutchins. Maybe because she was a conduit for malevolent energy. Or maybe because she was in touch with forces that would have rocked the complacent bourgeois worldview of the locals. How do *I* know? Also, even though the obit names her parents, I googled and looked around all over, and I can't find any other mention of them anywhere. Also, dudes, there's *no birth certificate* for Amy Madden."

Bud and Sally each made the same face. Obviously there was a birth certificate. Cory just hadn't found it, was all.

"Bud," ventured Sally, "it *is* sort of weird that she died in front of your house, and that she's come up a few times. I mean, I'm not suggesting there's really something supernatural going on!" Sally's forced laugh was basically a confession that she felt jazzed about such a possibility. "But it's fun to think about, right?"

Bud nodded. Totally neutral. "Sure." He stood up. "You guys want some beers?"

70

Her face flushed. "Uh, yeah, if you're having one, I guess."

Cory flung out his hands. "Dude, aren't you listening?! You're *haunted*!"

"That's nice, Cory. Hey, when's your festival? How long are you staying in Hutchins?"

"I'm sure as shit not leaving now," Cory snorted. "I'm telling you, this Amy Madden shit is the real deal. I think Fate's whole point in bringing me here was just to tell me in a roundabout way about Amy Madden."

Bud's bland composure broke. He stopped on the way to the kitchen and glared at Cory, face crisp with disgust. "*Fate'?!*"

"Yup. This is my destiny, dude."

"Okay, well, if you're going to pursue your destiny while you're sleeping in my guest bed and eating out of my fridge, please do it quietly. I didn't mind listening to your kooky shit during the weekend, but I didn't realize it was going to bleed into the rest of our lives." He indicated Sally with a nod. "And please don't keep bugging my, my friend with this stuff."

"If you want me to leave, dude, that's totally cool. I'll just mosey out to a bench in the local park, and always be grateful for the time you did let me stay. If I need to sleep on the streets in downtown Hutchins, that's no biggie, I've done that sort of thing before."

Bud dropped his eyes. "No, that's cool," he muttered, "no one wants you to sleep in the street."

"But if you do need to kick me out, just give me a few hours to set up a meditative divining."

"A what?" Bud no longer sounded annoyed, mocking, affronted, or confused. Just tired.

"I, like, have the ability to sink my consciousness into a trance and transform my soul into sort of a divining rod. I just need time alone to concentrate in the space I'm investigating beforehand. That would basically be the street in front of your yard. Once I'm in that, like, divinatory state, I'll be able to more clearly discern any weird wrinkles in the local reality."

"Oh you will, will you. Where did you develop this ability?"

"I've never actually *done* it yet. But I've read up on it, plus generally I'm a pretty experienced meditator anyway."

"Got it. Well, anyway, sorry. Permission denied. We're not turning my house into a base-camp for your spiritual escapades."

"Up to you, man. It would be a lot more comfortable and maybe more productive if I could go into the trance on your front porch. But if I have to do it sitting on the sidewalk, I'll manage."

"I'll call the fucking cops if you do that hippie shit in front of my house!"

"Sidewalk's public property, dude."

There was something humiliating about Bud's inability to rattle Cory. He'd always assumed that, at the end of the day, he was the strong one, and that if he ever really told flakey Cory off, it would crush the guy. But no, guess not. Bud stormed off into the kitchen.

After he'd rounded the corner, Sally stood and followed him. She found Bud standing motionless in front of the open fridge, staring into it as if lost. He didn't seem to hear her approach, or maybe he was ignoring her. She stepped closer and said, "Hey, Bud. Everything okay?"

He turned and blinked at her—jeez, he really *hadn't* known she was there. "Oh, yeah, Sally. Sure, sure. You want a beer?"

There was something spacey about him. Sally told herself he must really be upset about their pursuit of this Amy Madden stuff; but then she asked herself if he might be distracted by something else altogether. The look in his eyes was just so far away from her. He didn't seem pissed off by *her*, in particular, or by anything *she'd* done. Even so, she said, "Hey, listen. If it really bothers you for me to be nosing around all this Amy Madden stuff, then, you know...." A sudden rebellion kicked up inside her before she could relinquish the quest. She finished lamely with, "Then we can definitely talk about that."

But Bud only shook his head, lightly, distractedly. He kept peering into the fridge, as if searching for the beers that were right there before him. "No, that's okay," he said. "I doubt you'll find her."

# Eleven

But she was not so difficult to be found as all that; not anymore, not at the moment. She had begun to surge up out of the background noise of creation, her pattern forming and manifesting lustily in the flesh-and-mud world. Not everyone would receive a visitation; nor would all who sought her succeed; but the odds of running into her were better than they'd been at any other time since her death.

Amy Madden had been part of Hutchins High's class of '97. Sally herself had gone to that same school with the class of 2007. Being separated by a decade, it was no surprise she'd never heard of Madden. How wild would a student have to be for tales of her to circulate after all those years, at an intensity sufficient for them to filter down from the teachers, through the social bedrock separating them from the students? But students getting killed by cars were rare enough that Sally bet the memory of it had lived on.

Back in high school, Sally had been her eleventh-grade English teacher's pet, to such a degree that she even used to go see Mrs. Pierce at her house. Not so much when she was actually her student, but starting from the summer after her eleventh-grade year, and stretching all the way into her sophomore year of college, Sally used to pull up in Mrs. Pierce's driveway unannounced and ring her doorbell, with the brazen social effrontery of adolescence.

Now she pulled into that old driveway once again, as if all the intervening years had collapsed into nothing. For a moment she froze, sitting in her car, remembering back when she'd been the star pupil, instead of the dead-end manager of a Barnes and Noble.

Finally she propelled herself out of the car. Best to get to the doorbell and ring it before Mrs. Pierce or Dr. Pierce happened to glance out the window and see her loitering there, like a creep. As she climbed the porch steps she reflected that one effect of digging around in the whole Amy Madden thing was this sort of reconnection. Getting back in touch with Mrs. Pierce, as well as going to the library, going through the yearbooks of bygone days. Like she was reconnecting with Hutchins itself (or, well, *connecting*, for the first time).

Silence followed her push of the doorbell. Sally had the compulsion to turn and run, to treat the silence as permission to extricate herself from this socially unprecedented situation. But then she heard movement within. The big wooden door was yanked open and Mrs. Pierce stared at her through the glass of the porch door. At first her face conveyed only mildly confused, wary curiosity, no trace of recognition. Mrs. Pierce seemed to have shrunk somehow—her hair had gotten grayer, and a little wilder than in the old days. Back when Sally had been in school, Mrs. Pierce's hair and clothes and makeup had been immaculate.

"Hey, Mrs. Pierce," said Sally, putting on a grin. She waited a moment, and was about to give in and explain who she was when Mrs. Pierce's face opened up and brightened a bit—it didn't shine with the gladness with which she'd greeted Sally in the old days, but then again maybe a lot of that brightness had only been Sally's imagination. Anyway, Mrs. Pierce said, "Sally," only needing a moment's pause to recall the name. "Wow. What have you been up to?"

"Oh, nothing much."

She waited, with her pasted smile. Finally Mrs. Pierce shook herself and said, "Come in, come in!," opening the door wider and stepping aside.

Sally entered and headed for the living room, falling automatically into the pattern of her old impromptu visits. Some of the furniture and knick-knacks had changed. Sally was surprised to see the cliché hold true, to find that the room really did seem smaller. Mrs. Pierce slipped around her and into her habitual armchair, the one with the floral print. As she had many times before, Sally sat in the matching loveseat. Once they were both settled Mrs. Pierce gave a start, as if she'd just remembered part of the ritual; "Would you like me to get you something? Something to drink, maybe?"

"Oh, no, I'm fine."

"You sure?"

"I'm sure."

"Well. This is a nice surprise. How have you been? Still writing?"

The idea that there might be people who thought she still wrote threw her for a loop. She'd given that up her sophomore year of college. Her mouth hung open a few seconds before she found words to put in it: "Not really, no."

"Oh." Mrs. Pierce slumped back in her chair, disappointed. "Well. It's never too late to get back into it."

In Mrs. Pierce's mind, she was still that talented student who toyed with the idea of becoming a writer someday. Sally felt like an imposter. "Yeah," she said. "And what about you? How are you doing? How's Dr. Pierce?"

"Fred passed away." She said it as if surprised that Sally hadn't already known.

"Oh. Gosh, I'm so sorry." Memories of Dr. Pierce flashed behind Sally's eyes: the scurrying, mild-mannered way he would duck his head, the sad tension in his shoulders that sparked amused tenderness but also (let's be honest) a certain contempt. She waited to see if Mrs. Pierce would explain how and when he'd died. But Mrs. Pierce only sat there. Sally blushed, unsure how to fill the silence.

Perhaps the need to change the subject gave her an extra push. In any case, she had a sudden inspiration on how to broach the topic of Amy Madden. "I have kinda-sorta been working on this project."

"A writing project?"

"I think so. I'm not totally sure yet what it's going to wind up being."

Mrs. Pierce looked intrigued, and almost desperate, as if she'd been sitting in this tastefully decorated room in this big house for a long time, waiting for something to knock her off the track she was running on. "Tell me about it."

"Well. I'm kind of still in a research phase. But I've sort of been looking into this girl called Amy Madden."

Sally had expected a blank look from Mrs. Pierce. Even if she did remember Amy Madden, it ought to take her some time to rummage around in her head for the memory. After all, the girl had died in 1997, over twenty years ago. But Mrs. Pierce's face crisped and blanched in a way that let Sally know she perfectly well remembered her. "What are you looking into *her* for?"

Sally stammered, taken aback. Finally she managed a truncated account of the synchronicities that had popped up around Amy Madden; she left out the churning head and the barfed fish, but told her about the vine-clogged grave, the half-formed alchemy-related rumors Cory had picked up on, and the coincidence of where she'd died. As a foundation for some sort of rational investigation into something going on in the real world, it sounded crazy. But as she listened to herself Sally discovered that, as the impetus for some kind of vague artistic project, it sounded absolutely convincing.

Not that Mrs. Pierce seemed impressed. "Well," she said, pinching off the word with pursed lips. "Even with all that, if I were you I'd look for someone besides Amy Madden to do your project on."

"But … why?" Mrs. Pierce had said that as if Amy Madden were a bad influence she shouldn't be hanging around with, instead of a girl who'd been dead for decades.

"Frankly, because she was a bitch. A toxic little bitch." She said the last word with a peculiar catch, as if she had to muscle through some vestigial taboo against referring to her charges as bitches, especially in front of one of their number. "In all the years I spent teaching, she's the only one I ever…."

The sentence crumbled apart, and Mrs. Pierce shut her mouth. Sally wondered what she'd been about to say, then realized what it must have been: "the only one I ever was glad to hear had died," or something like that.

The sentiment chilled Sally. But it did not exactly lessen her interest in Amy Madden. "To be honest, that makes her even more fascinating. To write about, I mean." Lamely, she added, "I mean, it's not as if she can come after me for writing about her, right?," then vaguely regretted the quip.

Mrs. Pierce didn't reply at first. Just kept staring at Sally while seeming to see something else, that sour look puckering her face, hands gripping the armrests, legs crossed tightly and foot kicking in a nervous rhythm. Any good feelings about reuniting with her old pet seemed to have dissipated.

Sally tried prompting Mrs. Pierce: "What was it about her that was so toxic?"

Mrs. Pierce made an odd, ill-defined gesture, more like an irritated spasm.

What a strange let-down, to come see Mrs. Pierce again after such a long time, and then not have it be a happy reunion. Sally considered toning it down, dropping the subject for a while and devoting some time to chit-chat. But she couldn't muster the bullshit. What she cared about was Amy Madden. It made her a little sad not to care more about good old Mrs. Pierce, not to see that rapport, that bit of her youth, come back to life again. But there it was.

"Did Amy Madden have, like, scholarly interests?"

Mrs. Pierce threw back her head and laughed.

Sally grinned. "I guess that's a no." She chose to take the laugh as an indication that they were once again friends having a good time, even though it was plainly a mirthless, bitter laugh.

"An emphatic no." It was still jarring to hear Mrs. Pierce's hostile contempt for this student; again, a student who'd been dead for decades! "I don't know where you got that. Are you sure we're thinking of the same person?"

"Pretty sure."

"Well, believe you me, you can find better things to do with your time than investigate that bitch."

Some of Mrs. Pierce's disdain for Amy Madden seemed to be infecting her feelings for Sally. It made Sally defensive. "Well, I don't know, she must have at least been interesting. I mean, you certainly still have strong feelings about her after all these years!"

"Hm. Anyway. No, I would not say her interests were scholarly. The only thing I ever saw her reading was that damn comic book. *The Apothecary.*"

"You remember the name of the comic book she used to read?"

"She had a copy with her constantly. She was always reading it, at lunch, in class! I had to take over Frank Garwin's class once, the day his father died. I went in there during my prep period. And that little tramp was in there, slouched in the back, her nose in that stupid comic. I told her to put it away, and she just *looked* at me, like … well, anyway. I let it go for a while. Then, finally, I said, 'Miss Madden, I'm asking you for the last time to put that comic book away.' And she just *looked* at me again."

Mrs. Pierce fell silent, grimacing into her lap, plucking at her fingers. She seemed embarrassed. At having let herself be stared down by Amy Madden? Sally waited, at a loss. When Mrs. Pierce didn't continue, she squirmed, and said, "Well, okay, but I mean, that sort of thing must have happened all the time, right? I mean, confiscating things from rowdy kids. How come you still remember this one incident so vividly, from almost twenty-five years ago?"

Mrs. Pierce waved her hands, as if it would be useless to try to explain.

She asked, "Do you remember her being into alchemy?"

Mrs. Pierce pulled her head back into her neck like a turtle and made a face like she most definitely did not remember that.

"Do you remember anything about, like, her family life?"

"I really don't," Mrs. Pierce said. Then she added, contradicting herself, "Her birth was fishy. Her so-called 'father' couldn't have been. He was in traction, in the hospital, right around the time she would have been conceived."

Sally's mouth fell open. "How do you know that?"

Mrs. Pierce shrugged. "Town gossip."

Sally's mind reeled at the notion that Hutchins had ever been bound together by anything as organic and strong as "town gossip." Lots of people would have had to know each other really well for that to work, right? Like, there would have to be plenty of genuine face-to-face socializing? "But, like, who told you the gossip?"

Mrs. Pierce frowned. "I don't remember."

"Well, do you remember, like, when you learned it? Like, under what circumstances?"

Mrs. Pierce threw up her hands. "No! It was a long time ago! *I* don't know, maybe it *isn't* true!"

Sally thought Mrs. Pierce seemed rattled that she couldn't remember where this knowledge had come from, Like, maybe it wasn't true knowledge after all. Maybe she was startled to realize what a flimsy, possibly illusory foundation her ideas about Amy Madden rested upon.

Or maybe she was just embarrassed to have been caught being so small-minded as to blame a girl for the alleged adultery of her parent. It *did* strike Sally as petty, and made her feel embarrassed for Mrs. Pierce.

"I don't guess you know, like, if her parents are still in town? Or anything like that?"

"No, I don't."

"Mrs. Pierce, there must be some reason why this girl stands out in your mind after all these years. It would be really helpful if you could tell me what that is."

"Listen, Sally, you should really just keep away from her."

"She's dead!"

Mrs. Pierce huffed and stared helplessly into a corner.

"Mrs. Pierce. Please. It's for my writing project."

Oh, well, in that case, if it's for a writing project.... The old teacherly habits must have roused themselves, because Mrs. Pierce folded her hands in her lap and composed herself, as if she'd blown off her steam and was prepared to cooperate. "All right," she said. "I'll tell you what I can remember." After a pause: "She was very promiscuous."

Okay. While Sally hardly expected her former teacher to be a champion of adolescent free love, she was taken aback by the prim disdain with which Mrs. Pierce loaded the accusation. "So she had, like, a lot of boyfriends?"

Mrs. Pierce's mouth twisted in pity at Sally's naïveté. "I wouldn't dignify them with that title."

"Okay, so she slept around with the students…."

"Not with the students."

Oh, wow. So Amy Madden had been fucking some teachers. Now things were getting juicier, although Sally still didn't quite understand the level and the longevity of Mrs. Pierce's rancor. "Um, I know it's not any of my business, but can I ask, um, who with?…"

She waited. Mrs. Pierce was blinking, hard. Her eyes were shining and turning red.

Finally, Mrs. Pierce said, "You're talking like she was just a problem at school. Usually, you have a terrible student, you can at least leave the school and at least try to put them out of your head. Nine times out of ten they're just kids, they're not really bad people. But then once in a while you get someone like Amy Madden, who's just rotten—although there never was anyone else as rotten as her, thank God. But even those, you hardly ever see outside of school, and eventually they either graduate or drop out and they're gone, you don't have to worry about them anymore. But Amy Madden was always there. I swear to God, I used to bump into her once a week, somewhere around town. And other people saw her and knew about her, people who weren't even involved in the school. Like, well, for instance…."

She paused and dabbed the tears from her cheeks with her sleeve. Sally held her breath. Dr. Pierce had been a dentist. She remembered her parents talking about how they'd almost picked Dr. Pierce to be the family dentist, instead of the Dr. Thorpe she'd grown up with. She wondered if Dr. Pierce had been Amy Madden's dentist.

Mrs. Pierce cleared her throat and continued. "Even my…. I had a, a friend who got mixed up with her, God knows how or why. He was not the sort of man you'd expect that of, I can

80

assure you. And in fact I'd say it really discombobulated him. Everyone thinks that in a situation like that, with an older man and a very young girl, that it's the man who holds all the power. Well, I know this isn't very politically correct to say, but that is *not* always the case."

Horror goosebumped Sally's arms. Fuck the writing project, fuck the paranormal investigation shit, she wanted to end this conversation. She nodded sagely, still pretending they were talking about some random middle-aged man. "Sure, I can totally see that. I mean, these kinds of things can get so complicated emotionally, no one from the outside really has the right to say whether the…."

"No," interrupted Mrs. Pierce, voice harsh as a scrape. "I don't mean anything like that. I don't mean she seduced him, I mean *he didn't want to*. He didn't want to and she made him do it anyway."

Sally sat still, unsure whether she was supposed to say anything. Mrs. Pierce's red eyes and slash of a mouth were like a challenge, daring her to call the claim into question. "How?" Sally asked finally, in a small voice.

"I don't know, he never could explain. But that's what he said, and I believed him. You could tell from the way he acted that it had broken him. You could tell if you really knew him, I mean. Before and after."

# Twelve

Ever since the nice date they'd had, Sally had become Bud's go-to masturbation fantasy; the fact that they actually did know and like each other added a certain tenderness and realism to the jerking off. But things had been left so awkward between them that, when he decided to kill time with a session, the vision of her left his penis soft and sad in his hand. So he walked to his laptop, slowly, because he had his pants and underwear around his ankles. As he booted up the Mac, he took an absurd, illicit pleasure in the feel of his bare ass cheeks pressing into the cool plastic mesh of his home office's ergonomic chair. You're not supposed to sit bare-assed in an office chair, yet here he was doing it anyway—ha ha ha! Although actually the people who designed and marketed these chairs must know lots of guys were sitting in them this way, for this reason. Was kinda what you'd expect from computer-bound men.

He scrolled through the thumbnail preview images on pornhub.com, distantly petting his penis, waiting for something to grab it. Nothing quite right here on this first page; frustrated, he narrowed the search using the key words "big tits," "blow job," and "two girls one guy." Dozens of new thumbnails replaced the old ones: pairs of busty women administering oral sex. He kept scrolling, kept petting. Still couldn't quite find the perfect thing. If any of these pairs had tried to go down on him in real life, he would have blown his wad before he even processed what was happening. But here on this digital smorgasbord, each set's charms were diluted by the endless options alongside them. These all looked like great blow jobs, sure, but if he kept scrolling he was sure to find the *perfect* blow job.

Weighing the merits of all these girls, he thought sheepishly of Sally. Her tits weren't even all that big, and yet it went without saying that he would rather be with her. They could have sex but also hang out and talk. If he did something goofy, like cum too fast or had a booger in his nose or accidentally poked her in the butthole instead of sliding it into her vagina when they were trying to do it doggy-style, then he sensed that she wouldn't hold him in contempt for it, that they'd be able to laugh about it together.

Yes, she was a cool girl. Maybe exactly the sort of girl that he should try to be in a real relationship with…. And yet, that old familiar part of his brain, that smirking, knowing part, uncertain, nervous, asked if this was really a good time to get mixed up with a girl like that? Not that anything was wrong with Sally, in and of herself. If he wanted to settle down someday, maybe it could be with someone like her (although was he maybe cheating himself by not holding out for someone more exotic?...). But could he genuinely claim to be ready to settle down? He'd only ever had sex with five girls; he'd always promised himself to at least reach double digits, and how could he make good on that if he planned on Sally being the last one ever? And then, take a look at all these double blow jobs, for instance. He'd been jerking off to double blow jobs ever since he'd been a kid, and was he never to have one for real? Ordinary people did have them, he felt sure. Obviously they were less common out in the world than on pornhub.com, but still. If he never got out there and seduced a couple of girls into sucking him off, didn't that make all the time he'd spent watching girls do so to other guys all the more pathetic? Naturally, such a seduction would be a well-nigh superhuman feat. But wasn't the very difficulty of the task part of what made it worthwhile? Wasn't its impossibility the very thing that would let him know, when he *did* accomplish it, that he'd at long last arrived in the upper ranks of manhood? As he clicked to the next page of thumbnails, he insisted exasperatedly to himself, for the millionth time, that the mere fact of never having had a double blow job did not make him a failure, that it was fine to limit his enjoyment of double blow jobs to the digital realm. But wasn't that exactly the sort of quitter's talk that a failure *would* use? In any case, he patently *was* a failure: he had failed to ever have a double blow job.

Look how cheerfully they went at it. He enlarged some of the thumbnails, not in expectation that any of these would represent the perfect pair he would eventually settle on, but just to see that expression so many of the girls shared, that uncomplicated yet slightly vicious good cheer. He had yet to evoke that expression on the face of any girl out here in the world of meat and time, had yet to even come up with the faintest plan of how he might do so. And was Sally the girl who would finally show him that face? He doubted it, he had to sadly admit. She would probably be able to show him many good faces, including many he hadn't yet imagined. But not this one that he'd set his sights on, so long ago.

It was his own fault. If only he'd been more of a man, earlier on. If only he'd gone out, grabbed life by the balls, and gotten his double blow job. If only he'd at least had a threesome already. If only he hadn't been such a perpetual pussy. Then maybe now he'd be ready for Sally. He would have already, like, sown his wild oats.

*I'm sorry, Sally,* he said, as he clicked on a leering, oily pair, one with a dick in her mouth and the other with a ball, and then as they jerked to life began to stroke himself in time to their ministrations.

His penis swelled under his fingers. From the speakers of his computer came cooing and an occasional spurt of laughing pleasure from the girls, as well as the smug moaning of the guy holding the video camera, unseen from the waist up. The speakers were pretty good, not the ones built into the computer but fairly high-quality little Bose speakers he'd hooked up. Still, the sound, pushing out at him from the speakers mounted just before his face, wasn't natural-sounding. It had that feel of a hollow core of silence encased in an amplified shell, that speaker-sound, which Bud had come to associate with sex over the course of untold hours masturbating in front of computers.

Except naturally the sound wasn't coming from straight ahead of him, not exclusively in any case. Wisps of it curled around behind him, to double back and encircle him. Sort of a sonic mimic, he supposed, of the cottony wisps of fog which were also encircling him. Surrounding him, and thickening, so that they cut off the rest of the room, till it was as if he were sitting inside a cloud. But the computer screen remained unobscured, the metronomic cooing of the oiled girls guiding the rhythm of his hand as his penis swelled and swelled. And the edges of the screen became wispy as well, tendrils of pixels breaking away and floating off to flank him, in order to ultimately, he knew, rejoin behind like two pincers. The pixelated flesh of the oily girls morphed and reconstituted, so that Bud just sort of melted into the understanding that the hand jerking his swollen dick was no longer his own, but that of one of the big-titty oily girls. Except, really, it was *ultimately* his, because the oily girls were part of him, they sprouted from his flesh; as for the blonde kneeling before him on his right, grinning in savage invitation, the curved talons of her left hand were only extensions of the striated muscle of the sweaty thigh they clutched, and where her right hand cradled his testicles, the pubic hair entered her palm as it entered his scrotum, traversing the lengths of both their bodies, branching off to crown and feet, and while they did remain pubic hairs they also were nerve fibers, transmitters of sensation. Same deal with the glistening brunette on his left; the fist that clutched and pumped his penis was ultimately indistinguishable from the penis itself; through the nerves that ran through his dick and into her palm he felt the chill of the air-conditioning on the back of her hand. Through his nerves he felt the excessive and steadily mounting lubrication of both vaginas, increasing in time with his own ridiculously large hard-on, which was beginning to resemble a granite balloon being blown up.

As in so many of the fantasies he'd been storing up for years, in each palm he cradled the fat jiggling tit of a different girl. And the really neat thing was that, simultaneously with the hand job, he was also getting titty-fucked, like, titty-fucked ten times at onces, because all his fingers and both his thumbs had changed into dicks. And now the blonde (or was it the brunette? he couldn't tell—they seemed to keep switching back and forth) came swimming up through the space between them, and opened her mouth to kiss him, and drew him into her mouth, and he disappeared into it.

Disappeared, as he was swallowed into the chasm of her moist hot black mouth, and then felt a squealing agony of pleasure that could not be prepared for as each atom was peeled back, flipped inside-out. He felt himself rearing up out of the shadows; the very darkness was also peeled back, inside-out, turning into a neutered, flat light. His vision floated up above his head, connected to his visual cortex by invisible nerves fashioned out of etheric tendrils, so that he could see his own body. Not that he really thought of it as "his" body, nor did he think of himself as "Bud;" the sensations and transformations had reached such a psychedelic pitch that questions of mundane identity no longer applied; his soul lacked enough purchase in this shifting terrain to hold onto such trivial, worldly afterthoughts.

Although the center of perception was concentrated now in this space floating above and over to the side of his body (his body which gave an impression of being colossal, though there was nothing nearby against which to judge its scale), he remained privy to every scintilla of sensation coursing through the body, somehow even more privy to it than if he'd been buried in its flesh. What with the screeching orgasms provoked merely by each square centimeter of flesh's friction against the antiseptic air, what with the horrible pleasure produced by the rubbing-together of arm against flank below the armpit, of the two thighs there at the crotch, his concentration kept getting knocked about so that it was hard to make out his own physical shape. But that information did gradually filter through: a squat, troglodytic, slope-browed and slope-shouldered form, belly pooching out in a slope, rooted in place like one of those banished Titans which remain, in a state beyond personality, eternally standing in their subterranean cachots. It was only natural that all perception should be organized in this elevated spot, instead of the face, since there were no perceptory organs left in the face. Eyes, ears, mouth, nostrils, all orifices had been replaced by quivering vaginas fringed with pubic hair that looked like eyelashes. And the ten digits of the hands, hands which right now were rising with a stately lack of haste to his face, were writhing prehensile dicks, whipping about like ferocious hungry tentacles.

At the sight of those rising penises, the personality called "Bud" started struggling to clamber its way back up to the helm, or else to pull the whole psychedelic structure of the soul back down to a level where a mere personality could manage it. Because Bud didn't want those dicks going into his face orifices. Never mind that he could feel, reverberating back from the potential futures, the ecstasy that such a face-fucking would produce, the unimaginable compounding of pleasures, penile plus clitoral and all that multiplied by the number of vectors available. The idea of those flailing dick-tentacles sticking themselves into those face-holes repulsed him. The notion of his eyes as slick vaginas disgusted him, and he rejected the notion of sticking a dick into his own eye on principle, regardless of whether the rejection was a matter of prejudice on his part.

Was he sure, absolutely sure, that he wanted to reject such pleasure? The chance would never come again…. Yes, goddammit, he was sure, he insisted, exasperated, still working to wrench those finger-dicks back down, back under his control.

He'd thought that last query had come from himself, from a moment of self-doubt. Too late he realized it had come from without, and had been more in the line of a warning.

Too late—he tried to scramble back into that vagina-eyed, dick-fingered body, still not sure he could withstand the genderless pleasure-pain of the self-fucking, but sensing that it would be a better option than what was coming instead. Too late. The vaginas withered and closed, the dicks dried up; the colossal, cretinous body shriveled down, down, down till it was only human-sized, maybe smaller.

And behind him reared a figure with perfect tits, a baseball cap, and a shlong that in a world of ordinary physics would be too heavy for her frame. Bud shrieked as he was pierced, soundlessly, because there was no air here for sound waves to travel through. He'd been given his chance, something informed him, not deigning to use words. He could have been a partner in the production of pleasure. But since he didn't have the stomach for that, he would be the mere raw material in its production. He screamed and screamed, trying to find and pass through the membrane on the other side of which the pain would transform into pleasure. Trying to find it.

# Thirteen

When Sally arrived at Bud's, the blue of the sky had grown deep. She parked at the curb and sprinted to his front door to ring the doorbell. Gone were all her earlier misgivings about how Bud was taking this little investigation, forgotten in the flush of having actually achieved results. Even the sadness she'd felt after her visit to Mrs. Pierce had faded. She had a genuine mystery that she'd made bona-fide progress on.

But those doubts came back as the doorbell went unanswered. She stepped back into the front yard and looked up at the house. A light shone from a second-floor window, but maybe he'd left and had just forgotten to turn it off. Sally tried to remember if they'd actually made plans to hang out this evening. Mortified, she wondered if she was being clingy and annoying.

Resentment of that embarrassment spurred her to go look in the backyard—maybe he was in the pool and just hadn't heard her. She walked around to the back gate and poked her head into the backyard. "Bud?"

"Sally?" Sally jumped; Cory was squatting with his back against the wall of the house, on the other side of the gate and just to her left, too low for her to have noticed him at first. "Yo, dude. What's up?"

"Um. Just looking for Bud."

Cory nodded. "Yeah, me too. But he doesn't want to let me in." Cory said it as if people not wanting to let him in was just an occasional fact of life.

"So he's actually here?"

Cory nodded again. "You can open the gate and come back here, instead of leaning over it like that. It isn't latched. Or you can just go ring the doorbell. I'm sure he'll let *you* in."

"No, I already tried that."

Cory scrunched his eyes up at her, suddenly concerned. "Really? You rang the doorbell? Did he know it was you?"

"*I* don't know if he knew it was me. But we had plans to see each other around now." Sally still couldn't remember if that was actually true, but she felt compelled to justify her presence. Mustn't look needy and pathetic in front of Cory.

"That *is* weird." He got to his feet and began walking away from the gate, toward the deck and the main bulk of the house. "Come on," he said, without turning to look at her.

She hesitated, reluctant to violate the sanctity of private property, and afraid that Bud would get pissed at her for snooping. The Amy Madden game didn't seem worth that risk, since it wasn't like she really *believed* in any of this. But in the end she opened the gate and followed Cory. "You're sure he's actually home?" she whispered, as she climbed the steps onto the deck.

"Dude, why are you whispering?" Cory put his hands on his hips and leaned back, looking up the tall exterior of the house. "Yeah, totally. When he wouldn't answer at the front door, I came around here and started yelling for him. His bedroom window is that one up on the second floor, on the right. Anyway, the light's on up there, like you can see, and I saw him moving around in front of the window. I figured he must've heard me, so I gave up hollering for him and went and sat by the gate. And that's where you found me."

Sally gave him the silent side-eye, wondering about a person who would just hop around to the backyard and start hollering for someone who had declined to let him in the front door. Then again, all his stuff was at Bud's and he had nowhere else to go in Hutchins. Anyway, *she* was sneaking around to the back because no one had answered her in the front.

Cory went to a narrow window and pushed it open. The first-floor bathroom window. Sally's heart started beating faster. "Uh, should you be doing that?"

"Don't worry, it isn't locked. Can you give me a hand up?" He pulled himself up to the sill. "Never mind," he said, wriggling his way in.

Sally waited. She felt prissy and hypocritical for being so scandalized by Cory's break-in, while simultaneously waiting for him to let her in so she could profit off it. He came around, unlatched the sliding glass door, and slid it back for her.

She stepped across the threshold, and whispered, "Let's just make sure he's all right, then leave him alone."

Cory gave her a serious look, which felt all the more foreboding for being out of place on his features. "So you feel like he's in trouble, too?"

Sally didn't reply. She hadn't felt that, exactly, until Cory said so. Cory advanced into the living room, switching on lights as he went. At the bottom of the stairs he called up them, "Bud?! Hey, cuz, you up there?! How you doing?!"

From upstairs came a sort of annoyed, snarling groan, then Bud called down, "Jesus, Cory, how'd you even get in here? The fucking doors are locked."

"Yeah, but you left the bathroom window open. Dude, are you all right?"

The sound of Bud's footsteps, coming down the stairs. Sally had the ridiculous urge to hide behind a sofa before he caught her here, before he realized what a nosey, clingy, needy girl she was and decided he didn't have time to waste on someone who couldn't respect his basic privacy.

Sure enough, when Bud descended the stairs far enough to see her, the dismay on his face took on a new dimension. "You, too?" he accused, wearily.

"Sorry." Then, hating herself for her cowardice: "Cory was coming in anyway, so I figured I may as well, too."

Bud looked like shit. Ashen, with crimson blotches and a sheen of perspiration. Cavernous shadows under his eyes. Concern for him smudged away the obscure hurt she felt at being lumped in with Cory. She took a step towards him, not wanting to get too close, in part because she didn't want to display her emotion in front of Cory, in part because she could feel an unwelcoming vibe emanating from Bud.

But that vibe in and of itself wasn't going to keep her away, she realized. Even if it meant annoying him to the point that he didn't want to see her anymore, she was going to stick around until she'd made sure he was at least not super sick. She guessed that meant she really cared about him.

While she was trying to think of a diplomatic way to broach the subject of his appearance, Cory said, "Dude, you look like garbage. You feeling okay?"

"No. But that's none of your business."

"Well, maybe if we all sit around and pool what we've learned about Amy Madden it'll help you feel better. I always feel like making progress in a, like, intellectual pursuit takes my attention away from my body problems."

Anger clotted Bud's face at the mention of Amy Madden. "Cory, I haven't made any 'progress' on Amy Madden, and I don't feel up to sitting through your bullshit!"

It was like Cory hadn't heard the second part. "That's cool, dude, maybe Sally made some progress, and I have some ideas too. You can just sort of listen tonight. You don't have to make some big contribution every single time we talk about her."

Bud put his hand over his eyes. Sally considered keeping her trap shut; instead, she said, "I actually have made some progress."

Cory turned and gave her an enthusiastic grin. "Hey, that's great! Tell us about it!"

"No, don't." Bud was looking at her from under his brows, his whole body slouching forward and his head bowed. His expression was a more sour, sullen version of the look he'd given her when he'd said *You, too?* "I like you, Sally. But, you know. With Cory, it's different. He's family, plus we've known each other forever, so up to a certain point I have to put up with his shit. But you and me … I mean, we barely even know each other. So I really don't have to, with you."

Sally blinked back tears. "Yeah. Okay." She couldn't decide which stung worse, the ominous finality of his words or her own stupidity. He had every right to kick her out, to dump her. She *had* basically broken into his house, after all … well, Cory had, but she'd been complicit. He'd asked her to back off and she'd refused, and since, like he said, they really didn't know each other, why should he put up with it? She'd let herself start thinking of them as a couple, and so she'd allowed herself the sort of liberties people can take with a partner, when they're in a couple. And because she'd let herself start thinking that way, this didn't merely feel like being asked to leave by a guy she'd been on a couple dates with (actually, come to think of it, they'd never really been on a *date*). It felt like a real break-up. And she felt the same hurt, angry, ashamed betrayal as every other time she'd been dumped. It had been a long time since she'd been in a relationship serious enough for its end to qualify as getting dumped, but the pain remained familiar. Only this time it hurt worse. Maybe because there was something special about Bud, or maybe because this time, she was so much older. "That's cool, whatever you want. I'm sorry, I didn't mean to offend you."

She started to turn, to begin her mournful progress back to the sliding door. Before she completed the motion she yelped and jumped, jerking back around to stare wide-eyed over Bud's shoulder, breath heavy, her whole body sprouting goosebumps.

Her wild motion made Bud jump. "Jesus! What is it?!"

Cory glanced in the direction she was staring, then gave up when he saw nothing and took a step towards Sally instead. "Did you see something?" he demanded.

If it hadn't been for that look he gave her, she might just have said *Oh, nothing,* and continued on her way out. But whatever had just happened, Cory took it seriously, and that gave her pause. Prompted her to take a couple of seconds to digest the experience, instead of shedding it as quickly as possible. And in digesting the experience, she found that it pissed her off.

Something had been leering behind Bud, on the stairs. Some not-quite-humanoid smudge of heat. Leering over his head, at *her*, to taunt her. Much as she would have liked to claim altruistic, heroic motives, maybe the most immediate reason for her anger was not the danger to Bud which she somehow intuited, but that the threatener should taunt her so gratuitously, when she was already on her way out the door.

There was some fucking bitch up there with him.

"Did you see something?" Cory asked again.

Bud had his hands up. His fingers pulled and twisted at his collar. It made him look like a cross between a crying child and someone saying the rosary. "Yeah, did you?" he asked.

The fear in his voice infected her, but also stirred her protective instincts. And her will to fight. Instead of coming out and answering their question, she said, "Yeah, I did dig up some stuff on Amy Madden. A pretty destructive bitch."

"Destructive," repeated Cory, in a prompting tone.

"Yeah. Like, a homewrecker for one. Pretty promiscuous."

Cory's intensity diffused, and he looked almost embarrassed on Sally's behalf. "Oh, well ... I mean, that's not really, you know...."

"No, that's not exactly it," said Sally, frustrated at not being able to quite express it. "It was more like...."

The rest of the sentence was dashed from her brain by a wave of sensation. Below her was Fred Pierce's round, gray-haired, scarlet face, forty-something, younger than she'd ever seen him in life. His features puckered in terror, his eyes rolling back in orgasm. She squeezed the penis clamped in her vagina, pinched with her dirty broken nails her own tits, tits bigger than any Sally'd ever had before, and laughed, even if the sound was only in her own mind.

Back in Bud's house, she howled, spasmed away from where she'd been standing, stared around with her hands twisted into claws, snarling at the violation she'd just suffered. Bud took a step toward her then stopped, cowering, pointedly not turning to look at the place on the stairs behind him that had scared Sally, as if he knew there was something there and refused to look because he didn't want to have to admit he knew it. Cory had adopted a wide-legged stance, arms spread out, fingers extended, eyes darting as he tried to follow what was happening.

Sally tried to catch Bud's eye. He avoided hers. "Bud, she's really here. Isn't she?"

"You're the only girl in the house, Sally."

"You guys, uh, you guys can see her?" Cory asked. "Amy Madden? Like, is she a ghost?" After so many years of chasing kooky stuff, Sally imagined it must gall Cory to finally be in the room with a real heavens-to-betsy ghost and be the only one unable to perceive it.

Except Sally hadn't exactly *seen* it, either. And she felt unsure that it was a "ghost," exactly. "Bud, we can't stay in this house. Come with me, out to the car. We'll go."

Bud shook his head, eyes shining with tears. "You don't believe in this stuff, Sally."

True. She didn't. But the genuine experience of Amy Madden's consciousness forcibly violating her own made her beliefs or disbeliefs a moot point. "Just come with me anyway, Bud."

His eyes squeezed shut and his mouth opened wide, real wide. A high-pitched squeal emitted from him; for a second Sally thought he was going to cry, like a scared little boy. But then the squeal kept intensifying till it became a real cry of pain, and she saw a reddening patch of flesh elongating from his neck, as if being pinched and pulled by invisible fingers. "Sally!" Bud screeched. "You and Cory get out of here, please! Or else she's gonna take it out on me!"

Sally gaped, not quite comprehending. Cory put his hands on her shoulders, ushering her out; "Uh, okay, looks like we better get going...."

She shuffled along with him, mouth still open. "Shouldn't we stay and, I don't know?..."

"Dude, I seriously think she's gonna take a chunk out of his neck if we don't get a move on."

He was right. The flesh was more distended now than she would have thought possible; blood dripped down his neck where it was starting to tear. Bud clamped his jaw down to stifle a scream, and waved at them furiously to go. "All right," Sally muttered, "you win." She didn't speak loud enough to be heard, but she had a feeling even her thoughts were audible to the entity in the house.

Maybe out of habit, Cory led them out the front door instead of back the way they'd come. Before closing the front door behind him, he called into the house, "Hey, dude, don't forget to lock the sliding door, we left it open!" Then, the door shut, he and Sally stood on the porch staring at each other. Even though the confrontation hadn't made any noise to speak of, being cut off from it so suddenly had the effect of an abrupt silence. During their brief time inside the sun had slipped the rest of the way below the horizon.

Sally felt uncertain and a little silly. "That didn't just happen, did it? We had some sort of hallucination, right? Or that thing that happened to Bud's neck, maybe it was a hematoma or something."

"We're out of her influence now, so you're reverting back to your usual thought-patterns. But when we were in there, you felt her. You couldn't think the way you usually do, her presence wouldn't let you. Try to, like, remember that sensation."

Cory was right. It wasn't even a question of some imminent danger that had overridden her usual illusions. People died all the time because their ideologies blinded them to real-world dangers. No, it wasn't a question of psychology; more like the metaphysics of the room had shifted around her, so that while inside she had found it impossible not to believe in Amy Madden. Whereas now that they were outside, the metaphysics had shifted back, and she once again found it impossible to believe in such an entity, and equally impossible to recall how she'd ever managed to do so.

Sally looked at the heavy, mute front door, longingly. She hated and feared Amy Madden. But she also already missed *believing* in her, believing in her for real. She could see how one could get addicted to the experience. Was this the thrill Cory was always chasing?

"We can't just leave him here with her," she pleaded.

Cory shook his head, somehow managing to seem implacable

98

without shedding his usual lackadaisical air. "Don't worry. She's not gonna kill Bud; she wants him for something."

"How do you *know* that?!"

"Uh. Well, I guess actually I don't. But she *can* kill him if she wants, I think, so we had better keep from pissing her off until we can go after her for real. We're gonna have to, like, exorcise her."

"I beg your pardon?"

"Yeah, basically. Cast her off the mortal plane, or whatever. To do that we'll have to know more about her. The root of her power. Her modus operandi. That sort of shit."

They had left the porch; Cory had climbed down the front steps and was moving toward her car. Sally sensed that he did so mainly to draw her away from the house, and lessen the chances of her doing something rash. Probably a good idea; she couldn't think of anything she could do that *wouldn't* be rash. "What are you talking about, an exorcism? You and me? We're not fucking priests. What are we going to do, find some ancient pagan ritual to do on her? Where are we going to find it? In some ancient leatherbound tome they just happen to have on the shelves of the Hutchins Library?"

Cory gave her a gently patronizing smile. "Regular people always think that's how it works. Like, as if this is some *Harry Potter* movie where you just say some particular words in some fake-ass Latin and that's it, presto. But in real life the ritual comes from *within*. *You* create it. You just gotta be, like, open to the contours of the experience. Like, you gotta keep loose. And the really tricky thing is you gotta totally believe in what you're doing. Sure, it would be easy to believe in something you pulled out of some musty old encyclopedia, something that's been like totally sanctioned by a bunch of Oxford dons and Kabbalists and whatever. But believing a hundred-percent in something you know good and well you're making up on the spot—dude, that takes heart."

Sally couldn't believe she'd spent the last few minutes taking this guy seriously. "If we're just making shit up anyway, why do we have to learn anything more about Amy Madden? Why can't we just imagine what the root of her power is, and then believe in it really really hard?"

"Because if we haven't done any research and don't have any real-world struts, it'll be harder for us to believe in the ritual we make up."

Sally didn't reply, because she didn't know what to say. As she took out her keys and went around to the driver's side door, she looked up at the house again. She wanted to run away from it, hide someplace and never again think of Bud or the monster enslaving him; she also had an adventure junkie's urge to go back inside, to once again feel that thrilling metaphysical tilt, that stomach-jolting sensation of a new reality asserting itself. To Cory, she said, "You want to come crash on my couch, I guess?"

"Nah, that's cool. I'll go around back, sleep on the deck on one of the lounge chairs."

"What?"

"Oh, don't worry, I've done way worse. Couple weeks ago I was sleeping in parking lots in Dallas."

"You are so fucking *weird*. How can you sleep with that fucking ghost or whatever she is right there in the house?"

"Physical proximity or distance isn't, like, a factor. I mean, maybe on a bigger scale it is, but not here in town. I mean, think of all the places she's manifested. The graveyard, right? Plus during the thing with you and Bud and the head and the fish she was manipulating shit simultaneously at the mall and Bud's office, and those places are pretty far apart. I kind of feel like, either her attention is on me, or it isn't. Doesn't really matter where I sleep."

"You're a human, right? Like, with normal human nerves? Won't you be too freaked out to sleep here? Regardless of how you logic it out?"

Cory nodded, as if she brought up a reasonable point. But he said, "Thing is, though, I'm pretty tired."

# Fourteen

They fell into a strange new routine; in the end it lasted only three days, but it felt to Sally like a whole new way of life. One that might have been unbearable, if not for the capacity shared by any routine for dulling emotion, for softening the angles of reality. Every morning for three days Sally drove to Bud's, to pick up Cory. He insisted on continuing to sleep there, in the backyard. Sally liked to think Cory was staying at that literally haunted property as part of some plan (maybe he needed to be there in order to go into a "divinatory trance" each morning?), but she had the uneasy suspicion that he just found it easier than looking for someplace else to crash. Every morning she would drop him off wherever he wanted to go: the library the first day, the high school the second (*her* old high school—strange to think that it had been Amy Madden's school first), the center of old downtown the third. ("Old downtown" took up half a dozen square blocks. A few of the buildings did seem sort of quaint, but Sally had no idea how "old" they really were.) Then she went to work while he did whatever it was he did. The first day she went into the library with him and checked out every book they had on alchemy (there were two). At work over the next three days, she used her employee discount to buy thirteen books on the subject from their Self-Help & Occult section, earning herself some raised eyebrows. In the evenings, at home, she stayed awake into the small hours, studying the books, highlighting passages. At work, she stole as many moments as she could to flip through all the other books Barnes and Noble had that dealt with the subject, even in the most passing way, or to read up on it with her phone's Wikipedia app. It all seemed

101

like bullshit to her, but Cory claimed they had to learn all they could about the bitch before they took her on, and since the bitch supposedly fancied herself an alchemist, that must be a good place to start.

All things for Sally had become tinged with dark significance. Dimly, she realized that this was what she'd wanted, or something like it; she'd wanted the drab stupid world to assume layers of meaning. For instance, the oldish lady in the Tween section, standing up straight with her beak of a nose inches away from a Babysitters' Club book. Sally rounded the corner to stock the shelves, and the woman's eyes shot up and locked on her like she'd been expecting Sally to show. And she kept staring as Sally jammed the books onto the shelves and straightened them. Sally kept half an eye on her, warily watching for any occultish vibe. But the woman seemed like just another sad weirdo. According to Cory, they were supposed to be going by their gut feelings, and Sally's gut didn't tell her this lady had any significance.

She even confirmed that with Cory, during one of their morning drives. "There's a lady at work that seems kinda, I don't know…." She started to tell him about the strange Tween lady.

He cut her off: "Dude, I'm picking up on a lot of doubt in your tone. Do you really sense that this lady is linked to Amy Madden?"

"I *don't* sense it. But she is weird, though."

Cory shook his head. "Everybody's weird. I'm weird, you're weird. Weirdness isn't enough. You gotta trust your instincts, the truth you know way down deep. In a, like, endeavor like this one, you gotta kiss reason goodbye altogether. Because reason would tell you not to even attempt this shit. You may as well trust your feelings, because if it turns out we can't trust our hunches, then we're basically fucked no matter what we do."

Fair enough. She'd also had a strange dream about a guy named Kargloz, who lived in a sort of subterranean cave complex with fires spurting out of the ground all over the place. In her dream she knew his name, and that he was into alchemy.

But it felt like a mere dream, with the alchemy angle thrown in no doubt due to her recent obsession with the subject. She started to tell Cory about it, too. Again, his first question was whether she had a gut feeling that it was psychically significant, and when she said "no" he waved a hand, dismissing it. Fine. Wasn't like she had any dearth of strange dreams—they couldn't *all* be psychically significant.

Besides alchemy, the other thread she kept pulling on was Mrs. Pierce. Surely her old English teacher knew more than she herself realized. Surely she unwittingly held some clue. That first day, Sally finished work at three, and still had hours to kill before she was scheduled to pick up Cory. So she drove back to Mrs. Pierce's. Already this felt like a habit, too, like she'd picked up her old custom of dropping by Mrs. Pierce's unannounced, except that now the ritual was spoiled. When Mrs. Pierce opened the door and greeted her, it was not with the indulgent affection of a devoted teacher for her star pupil, but with the bitter dark rigidity of a woman trying to rise above a humiliation she cannot escape. And Sally felt her own face grow hot at the memory of Dr. Pierce's penis clasped in her vagina, of his frightened orgasmed face below her. She reminded herself that there was no way Mrs. Pierce could ever, ever guess that those alien sensations had been forced into her memory.

Even if Mrs. Pierce couldn't pretend to be glad to see Sally, she remained polite. "Would you like to come in?" she asked. Sally thanked her and stepped inside, feeling mildly guilty for accepting an offer that was so begrudgingly made. They progressed to the living room, just like old times. But all the warm feelings of those old times were gone, overwritten by this new reality that couldn't accommodate the old.

This second meeting didn't last very long. Sally kicked it off by mentioning Amy Madden's name, and right away Mrs. Pierce shut her down. "I really don't have anything to say about that girl," she said, her mouth muscles bunched and tight so as to prevent herself from saying something else. "I haven't even thought of her in over twenty years, you know."

Horseshit. "You really don't remember her being into alchemy?"

"I believe I just told you that I remember very little about her."

"It's just, there's a lot of weird stuff about her. Like, do you remember what she looked like? Somebody blurred out her yearbook pictures, and I haven't been able to find any other photos of her."

"Yes, I remember what she looked like. Perfectly well."

"Well … could you describe her? I'm sorry, I hate to keep bugging you like this, but it's just, my writing project…." It went on like that. Pulling teeth. "Was Amy Madden a total loner? Or were there any kids she particularly hung out with?" Maybe someone still alive and in Hutchins, that she could track down and interrogate.

Mrs. Pierce let out an unhappy, fake laugh. "You could at least pretend to show some interest in *me*, instead of diving straight into the third degree."

Sally felt ashamed and guilty, which only fed her anger. This shit was important, way too important to let Mrs. Pierce's personal feelings get in the way; of course, Mrs. Pierce had no way to know that. Sally gave her own, equally fake laugh. "I'm sorry, I know I keep blabbing about the same thing over and over. But I just can't help it. I'm obsessed."

"How on earth did you ever manage to get obsessed with Amy Madden, if you didn't go to school with her and never even met her?"

Thereby hung a motherfucking tale. Of course, Sally had already told it, the last time she'd been over. The sane version. She went ahead and reminded Mrs. Pierce about the mysterious vines that had sprouted and choked Amy Madden's grave; she shuddered at the dark satisfaction that squeezed Mrs. Pierce's features, at the thought of Madden's grave being defiled.

After more cajoling, Mrs. Pierce finally sighed and said, "All right, well, yes, I do remember a couple of girls that began hanging out with her. Two tall, pretty blondes. Long straight hair, and they dressed alike. Not the same exact outfits, but the same style. Sort of preppy. One day I just sort of noticed them trailing behind Amy Madden through the halls, and after that it seemed like they were always there. God knows what they saw in each other, they weren't types that normally would hang out together."

Sally asked more questions, but Mrs. Pierce shrugged them all off, unanswered. The girls possibly could have been twins, they had looked enough alike, but Ms. Pierce had the idea they'd just been sisters. If so, she didn't know how far apart in age they'd been—maybe one year? Maybe they *weren't* sisters. She had no idea of their names. She'd never had them in class, didn't remember having ever bumped into them in town, and would never have thought of them again if Sally hadn't insisted on dredging up all this Amy Madden nonsense.

Mrs. Pierce stood up. Sally felt a gnashing exasperation; Mrs. Pierce was still treating this like an interview she could simply end, because she had no idea of the stakes. To her, the main trauma was that Amy Madden had suborned and fucked her husband. Sally felt unreasonably frustrated at Mrs. Pierce's inability to understand that that shit was ancient history, that Sally wasn't here about poor Dr. Pierce, that Amy Madden was still around and was in fact a bigger threat than ever. She actually considered opening her mouth and saying so, but Mrs. Pierce cut her off: "Sally, listen. It's good to see you again." In her voice was the bitter acknowledgment that, in fact, it was *not* good. "But I feel like I've made it plain that I don't want to talk about that person. I'm glad you're writing again, and I wish you well with your project, but frankly I can't help you with this subject."

Mrs. Pierce made as if to say something more, but then stopped. By standing up and making her pronouncement with such finality, she'd left herself with nowhere to go except to ask Sally to leave. She would have liked to maneuver out of this cul-de-sac, Sally saw, because she really was very lonely, and it *should* have been a good thing to have Sally show up in her living room again. To have confirmation that her life had not been for naught, that this relationship she'd built still existed, that she needn't be all alone in the tasteful wasteland of this living room.

Sally couldn't help the two of them find a way out of this impasse. Under normal circumstances, she would have turned the cultivation of a renewed friendship with her old teacher into the major project of her current life, in order to watch in fascination as the relationship resuscitated and transformed into a friendship between two equal adults. But for now, she couldn't spare the energy to talk to Mrs. Pierce—or anyone else—about anything that did not pertain to Amy Madden. She stood, gave an apology that she didn't mean and that wasn't intended to convince, gave Mrs. Pierce a perfunctory hug, and left her old teacher there alone in her house, confused and blinking.

Not wanting to waste time by driving home, she parked her car in the Wal-Mart parking lot and spent almost three hours reading about alchemy till it was time to pick up Cory. They'd agreed to meet at this very Wal-Mart, so at eight o'clock she started the engine and drove to the front of the store to wait, letting the car idle. He was twenty minutes late. She asked about his progress, and he spouted on for a while. Sally thought that he sounded very enthusiastic for a guy who seemed to have accomplished nothing.

The next morning, the second day, she was waiting at the curb for Cory, engine idling, when Bud came out to his car. He paused, awkward, hesitant, then slunk over to her. He walked more slowly now than he used to, with a bow-legged old man's gait; around his waist and pelvis was a certain puffiness, as if he were wearing a diaper. She rolled down her window as he walked around to her side of the car. "Hey," he said, leaning in to put his head close to hers. A dark bruise blotched half his neck.

"Hey," she said. After trying to think of something better, she said, "How's it going?"

"Oh. Yeah. I don't know, really."

"Yeah…. This is, like, I don't know, such a weird situation."

Tension flowed from his body, in relief that she'd broached the true subject. "Yeah, you're telling me."

"I mean, it's just … I mean, so, you're possessed?…"

"No, no, no, I don't think that's the word. Because I'm still, like, *me*. I'm still basically in control of myself. Internally, I mean.

106

Externally, she … I mean, she sort of has her ways of imposing her will, I guess."

He tried to say this last bit with a light, sophisticated, ironic air, but she saw how the darkness clogged his features, and remembered that chunk of flesh being pinched from his neck, stretched, nearly torn off. Tortures were being enacted in that house. Now-familiar rage bubbled up within her, and a feeling of helplessness so desperate it was almost as if she, not Bud, were the one being regularly violated. Sally blinked back tears. "We're gonna figure out a way to get rid of that bitch, Bud. I swear it."

Bud flinched. She was quite sure he was stopping himself from looking over his shoulder, to check and see if Amy Madden was looming there. In a whisper, he said, "See, that's the thing. You guys are into this whole exorcism thing. But I'm afraid you're only going to wind up pissing her off. Whereas if we just let her alone, I think she'll move on eventually. She's just … I don't think she's the type to stick around till she's used people up completely. I think she gets bored after not too long, and then just drifts away."

As far as Sally could tell the bitch was still haunting her hometown nearly a quarter-century after her death, which didn't sound much like someone who moved on. Anyway, fuck it, moot point: "We're not gonna just leave you in her clutches, Bud. You're, you know…." She wanted to say *my boyfriend*, but couldn't get her tongue around the words and blushed instead.

"I'm just afraid you guys are gonna stir up the hornets' nest. I'm just worried about you guys making it worse on *you*." He added this last bit hastily, to cover up how obvious it was that, really, he was worried about himself.

His cowardice made Sally feel ashamed for him. She couldn't blame him, though. He looked up at something—she turned, and saw Cory walking over from his berth in the backyard. They all exchanged pleasantries. Bud signalled that the hellos were at an end by walking to his car, and as Cory was buckling his seatbelt Sally glided away from the curb, keeping a worried eye on Bud in the rearview mirror for a few moments.

She told Cory about Bud's concerns, but he only shook his head. "She's in a relatively harmless mood now, but all that could change." As usual, he gave the impression of having been through this sort of thing a hundred times and knowing just what to expect.

She considered calling in sick to work. But in order to do what? Work gave her a chance to turn over in her mind the reading she'd done the night before and this morning. Moreover, she reasoned that the routine and drudgery were helping keep her tied to the real world. If she holed up in her apartment with all those alchemy books and the sparse notes she'd scrounged up on Amy Madden, who knew into what rigid cocooned fantasies she might weave herself. The blandness of Barnes and Noble might help keep her mind limber. Maybe.

Not that Barnes and Noble wasn't getting weird, itself. That lady in the Tween section had become a regular, forever rigidly standing there with a Babysitters' Club book in her claws, right up against her face, and forever snapping her eyes onto Sally the instant Sally appeared. Sally tried not to rush to uncanny conclusions. It wasn't unheard-of for folks to show up, become regulars, and spend multiple days at the store without ever purchasing anything. For instance, Luke, with the shoulder-length gray hair, tight jeans, and cowboy boots, who showed up every day, sat in one of the store's complimentary armchairs, and read a Louis L'Amour paperback all the way through. But the old woman's ramrod posture was more unsettling than Luke's easy manner of flowing his body into the armchair.

Sally could have avoided the Tween section. Instead she began creating excuses to walk past it; the woman repulsed her, but she also felt compelled to keep checking if she was still there. And she was. How long could it take a grown woman to read a Babysitters' Club book? What would happen when she cycled through the whole series? She held the books so roughly in her claws that she was creasing the covers, and as a manager Sally really ought to have said something.

She remained convinced, for some obscure reason, that the strange lady was a mere coot, and not another manifestation of supernatural horror. However, she did have a dream about the lady.

In the dream she had decided to have it out, to challenge the oddball. She went and confronted the strange lady in the Tween section. But holding the woman's gaze, instead of immediately dropping her own eyes, allowed time for an unexpected process to unfold: the woman slowly lowered the book; her eyes seemed to grow larger, more bulbous. And the lower half of her face, her jaw and puckered mouth, seemed to shrivel, like her head's filling was being squeezed out of the lower half, and into the upper. Sally jerked awake, wondering what would have happened if she hadn't broken the connection. Would the lady's head have popped?

The next morning, the third, when she picked up Cory, she saw the curtain twitch in the second-story window of Bud's bedroom. She knew which room was his, though she'd never been up there. He was hiding from her. Hiding from *Sally*! After dropping Cory off (at the school, this time; he wanted to soak up the vibe of Amy Madden's alma mater), she tore off for Mrs. Pierce's, speeding, even running a stop sign for the first time in her life.

She pounded on the door till Mrs. Pierce opened it, mouth open, aghast. Before she could even speak Sally had pushed past her, into the house.

Mrs. Pierce glared as Sally fumed in the foyer, stamping around in circles. "I could call the police, you know. I could actually do that."

"I need to know about Amy Madden. Tell me something else."

Mrs. Pierce threw up her hands. "*What?* What in God's name do you want to know?! It's like you've gone crazy!"

It was indeed like she'd gone crazy. Started believing in ghosts and hauntings and demons and shit like that. Except, strictly speaking, it was the universe which had gone crazy, by suddenly allowing such phenomena. She was merely trying to keep up. "I need to know more about Amy Madden," she grimly repeated.

109

"What?! What?! What?! *What* do you need to know?!" Mrs. Pierce stepped up to her, got in her face. It hit Sally for the first time how much shorter than her her old teacher was. "I don't know why the hell you care about that *bitch*, and I *certainly* don't know what else you want me to tell you!"

Sally leaned her head down, till the women's noses were an inch apart. *"Supernatural shit!"* she roared. "You know good and damn well that I'm here for supernatural shit! I know you know something, otherwise you wouldn't fucking hate her so much!"

Mrs. Pierce recoiled, blinking at Sally in fear and betrayal. She couldn't believe Sally had come out and actually said it. "You really are crazy," she whispered.

"Fine. But you still know what I'm talking about."

Mrs. Pierce kept staring at her. Sally waited.

Nearly a minute went by. Then, in a dull hoarse voice: "He said she sat on his chest and took his breath."

Sally kept waiting. More was on the way. She let Mrs. Pierce build to it.

"She would suck the breath out of his mouth, and he said that while she did it his lungs stopped working and it was like he wasn't really alive anymore. And when she breathed his breath out through her nostrils, the mist turned to snakes and the snakes went inside him. I won't tell you where they went in at." Tears wetted her face. "And I won't tell you any more about that, period. Fred would be so ashamed if he knew I'd told you that much, he would never forgive me. I hope that's enough for your little *writing project*."

Sally couldn't meet Mrs. Pierce's eyes anymore. Now that she'd gotten all Mrs. Pierce had to give, she couldn't imagine what to do with it. She apologized. As she left they both said they would have to get together again sometime soon. Which was absurd, neither of them wanted to ever see the other again. It was like they were trapped in the reanimated corpse of a particular social situation, stuck going through its juddering motions.

She drove to Barnes and Noble on autopilot. Was so out of it, she'd already started working before she remembered she hadn't clocked in, and had to go back and do it.

Today she was part of the crew opening the store. After half an hour of getting things prepped, she unlocked the front door. Three early-bird customers were already waiting: two middle-aged women in Looney Toons sweatwear, and a small man with wisps of gray hair on his head and an untidy mustache. The Tween-haunting woman wasn't among them; that gave her a cold feeling. Because she felt sure that, now that the store was open, the lady would be at her post, regardless of whether she'd used a physical body to pass through the entrance.

Gone was her hunch that the Tween woman had nothing particularly supernatural about her. True, that did remain her subjective impression. And it was also still true that, as far as she could tell, she had nothing to guide her except her subjective impressions. But even so, she was starting to realize, her subjective impressions didn't mean shit. If her quest was important enough for her to go around tormenting people like poor Mrs. Pierce, then there was no excuse not to confront the Tween lady. And besides, Sally suddenly realized that some sort of switch had been thrown—now the lady oozed uncanny implications, and Sally knew, thanks to a little tickling voice in the bowels of her brain, that she had to be some kind of messenger from strange realms. Well, okay, it would be a stretch to say she *knew* that, but she definitely had a funny feeling. Those perceptions Cory had persuaded her to place such stock in had flipped. If she didn't rush straight to the Tween section, if she spent the first few minutes of the store's business hours with the usual rigmarole of assigning tasks and interacting with her workers, it wasn't because she was putting off the confrontation, but simply because a fatalistic calm had come over her.

Finally she had a free moment. For a few seconds she stood at her post, the customer-service desk in the middle of the store. Once she felt adequately present in her mind, she strode to the Tween section.

*Won't it be funny if today she's finally not there?* But she was, eyes snapping up to Sally's, talons man-handling the cover of her Babysitters' Club book. Sally felt relieved that she'd not yet missed her chance to hear the message, but also a sort of dismay that she wasn't going to get a reprieve.

Now that Sally held the eye contact, there was that same impression as in her dream of the lady's jaw shriveling while the top of her head swelled. Sally couldn't quite convince herself it was all her imagination, even though she couldn't really quite actually see it.

She'd resolved to wait out whatever happened, to just see what the strange lady would do. But as that not-quite-visible yet increasingly undeniable swelling continued, Sally's nerve faltered—she didn't want to get, like, splattered with brains. Right as Sally was at the point of saying something to break the tension, the strange lady spoke: "I didn't even want to *be* a babysitter."

Okay. Sally waited.

"I didn't want to, but my parents made me. They said I needed to learn responsibility. Value of a dollar. And I was too young to get a regular job. Only thirteen. So: the neighbor's kid. Amy Madden."

Sally felt a sickly wave ripple through her. "You were Amy Madden's babysitter?" But the age didn't add up. If she'd only been a few years older than Amy Madden, then she ought to only be around fifty now

The strange lady didn't reply, and Sally had to say something else to fill the air. She couldn't help it. "If you didn't like babysitting, then how come you read so many Babysitters' Club books?"

The lady blinked, trouble blurring her eyes behind the thick lenses of her spectacles. "I don't know anything else," she said. "I never had time."

The woman leaned forward, like a lonely stray. "I didn't want to, but my parents made me. They wanted me to learn responsibility. Value of a dollar. So: the neighbors' kid. And she sat on my chest."

Sally went cold. *You have got to be fucking shitting me.*

112

"She sat on my chest," repeated the lady, in an aggrieved, petulant voice, encouraged by Sally's interest.

"Who are you?" asked Sally.

"I'm Linda Middleton."

Sally's guts transformed into something very dense and cold. She immediately recognized the name from the girl's tombstone that Bud had showed her, that one day. "No you're not."

"She sat on my chest. I told my parents I didn't like her. 'Don't make me go over there. There's something wrong with that little girl. How she looks at me.' But they only got mad. They wanted me to learn responsibility. Value of a dollar. 'That girl is three years old,' they said. 'Stop being silly. You're only being silly.'"

"Who are you talking about?" asked Sally. "What little girl?" Because it couldn't be Amy Madden. This Linda Middleton was just too damn old to have been Amy Madden's babysitter.

Linda Middleton only blinked at her from behind her thick, distortive glasses. "But you know who the little girl was."

And Sally realized that the closer she looked at the lady, the blurrier and more indeterminate her age seemed. It was as if there wasn't much mass to her, as if her body were the dried-out, moulted shell of an insect, and at her core was only cheatedness, wasted time.

"So she sat on your chest," Sally said, slowly, carefully. One of her co-workers happened to be passing by as she spoke, leading a customer somewhere; he caught a snippet of the phrase and gave her a funny look. "But then what? What happened after that?"

The woman just stared at her, her bulbous and now unblinking eyes magnified by the eyeglasses. "Nothing's ever happened after that."

Sally wanted to find some way to mention the gravestone, without having to confess that she was entertaining unthinkable possibilities. "So, uh. Are you, um, any relation to the other Linda Middleton? That one who's buried out at Grandbled Cemetery?" And who *would* have been about the right age to babysit a toddler Amy Madden.

At first this Linda Middleton's face remained utterly blank, as if she hadn't comprehended the question. More and more, it got hard to think of the strange lady as *old*, exactly. More like she was deformed, in some subtle, obscure, fundamental way. Her flesh sagged, but maybe not with the weight of age; maybe as it would do if it had formed and grown in some place without gravity. Her eyes were bloodshot and rheumy, but maybe merely as the result of having spent long wastes of time in a lightless realm. Sally thought of cows that are bred and raised to be sold as veal, who are held all the years of their lives in cages too small to let them move, so as to keep their muscles soft. The meaning of Sally's question finally seeped into the woman's brain; her features scrunched in rage, and her eyes shot out a savage flurry of blinks. "My mom and dad come by there sometimes," she spat. "They don't know how it happened. I wish they *did* know, so they could know it was their *fault*! For sending me over there when I didn't want to go!"

She turned and stalked off. By the time Sally shook herself into action, the Tween woman had disappeared around a corner. "Hey!" cried Sally, and took off after her. At the end of the aisle she emerged into the open space of the store and stared around desperately, unable to spot her at first. Where the fuck had she gone?!

"There she is," said someone at her shoulder. Lance, a fellow employee. Sally followed his finger and saw Linda Middleton already on the other side of the store, waddling into the nest of shelves in the Fiction section. "You need back-up? She shop-lifting?"

"What? Jesus, no! Go back to what you were doing!" Sally hurried across the store after the woman.

She entered the Fiction section. Power-walking through the bookshelves she saw Linda Middleton flash by across a gap over to her right. Sally spun on her heel to follow. Next she caught a glimpse of her turning yet another corner, out of the Graphic Novels section. Impossible to have gotten there so quickly. Sally tried to follow; but the woman had disappeared. She rushed around, searching frantically enough that several employees tried to stop her and ask what was wrong (not Lance, who was sulking). She went to the front door and asked the security guard if anyone of Linda Middleton's description had left. (Nope.) She went into the ladies' room and checked under the stalls for the brown pumps Linda Middleton had worn, ignoring the stares of the women standing before the line of sinks in front of the mirror. (No dice.) She kept looking even after she was sure her quarry was gone. Sally had looked hard enough that she'd neglected her other duties; been rude to a few customers who'd tried to stop her with their dumb-ass questions; and had generally attracted enough attention that word would totally get back to her superiors. Oh, well, fuck it. Probably nothing would happen, and if it did, this was a shit-ass job anyway.

At loose ends, not sure what else to do, she wandered back to the last place she'd seen Linda Middleton. The Graphic Novels section.

If this had been a movie or a novel, she would have theorized that Linda Middleton was leading her to the Graphic Novels section on purpose. Showing her some clue. She went to scan the shelves there. And was dumbstruck to see that, unbeknownst to her, a new compilation had been placed on the shelves. A comic book called *The Apothecary*.

She drew the compilation off the shelf and began flipping through it. Triumphant understanding swelled up from low in her belly, but mingled with disgust. *All these ridiculous books I've been poring over,* she thought, remembering that dream of Kargloz which had felt so devoid of psychic significance. *All that New Age crap. Think of the time I could have saved if I'd come here first....*

She took the book to the front register and bought it, making sure the cashier remembered her employee discount. Then she went home sick. She told Lance she was leaving him in charge, then dashed away before he could say anything snarky.

# Fifteen

Over the past few days, Cory had surprised, even confused Sally with his apparent equanimity. He hadn't changed much in the few days since she'd met him, but the world had gone so topsy-turvy that quirks which had once seemed to border on mental disease now cast him as a bastion of strength. Everything had changed, except for him. Maybe that made him the most reliable person in the world. Except every once in a while she would remember how blithely he'd talked about garage tinkerers slapping together perpetual motion. Many times, as he sat beside her during these morning commutes, she wished she could see inside his head, if only to get a feel for how sane he actually was.

As Cory would be the first to admit, all he *really* knew how to do was wait. And how to have a good attitude about it. He considered himself to be basically a sort of divining rod. Every morning, waking up at sunrise on the deck's lounge chair, he asked himself what today's hunch was; one day it was the school, one day the cemetery, one day the small, ostentatiously, pre-fabricatedly quaint downtown. Only after he had this answer as to where he would begin the day's quest did he allow himself to get up and go take a leak on Bud's grass. Then he would sit in a lotus position and spend fifteen minutes or so in his divinatory trance. On only one of the three days did he see Bud to say hello, the morning Bud had been chatting with Sally. The guy looked like crap. Possession didn't agree with him. (Of course, Cory knew "possession" wasn't the best term; it would be more accurate to talk about an ectoplasmic co-habitation of a malignant nature.)

Three mornings, Sally dropped him off where he requested. From that starting point, Cory would wander, keeping his mind open and empty, clean of clutter, awaiting the slightest tug in any direction. Amy Madden's essence must suffuse this town, if there was enough of it to have generated actual psychophysical manifestations. So he wandered, eyes open like a child's, ready to catch the significance of any stray happening.

The process required trust and faith, all the more so since it was a process he'd basically made up. So, as he wound up his third miles-long, day-long trek, shuffling his way through the dusk back to Bud's home, he was reluctant to admit to himself the discouragement he could feel creeping in. Not doubt, he would not go so far as to say doubt. But after three days of not feeling so much as a quiver of an indication of how to delve into the deeper, sub-quotidian nature of Amy Madden and her powers, he would cop to a bit of discouragement.

It wasn't just these past three days; he'd spent years in search of the secret world. And not without results. He'd seen cool stuff, and enough circumstantial proof of the ubiquity of magic that he could only shake his head in compassionate, amused sympathy at all the people who thought he was full of shit. That having been said, he had always yearned for a *really* undeniable experience of the supernatural (or the chance to actually see a guy produce, say, cold fusion in his garage—same thing), and the wish had finally been granted the other night, when he'd definitely seen that invisible force pinch a chunk of Bud's neck. The concern he felt for his cousin and his jazzy excitement at getting to witness this phenomenon were not mutually exclusive.

And, while he honestly didn't think it would be cool to accuse him of anything so small-minded as jealousy, he had to admit to a certain wistfulness at the fact that, of the three people who'd been in the house that evening, he'd been the least affected, gleaned the sparsest sensory input. Bud had had direct physical interaction with the shade of Amy Madden, and Sally claimed to have actually had a memory of Madden's forced into her psyche, though she was strangely reluctant to describe it.

No, he would not call himself jealous, exactly. But he did hope that the next big manifestation would focus on him.

If Bud or Sally had been privy to this desire, they would have called him crazy; they would have gotten pissed at him for not counting his lucky stars that he'd escaped the spirit's notice. But to him, nothing could have been more natural than to want to make direct contact with Amy Madden and her milieu. Sure, it would be risky. But some shit was just so cool that it was worth the risk.

Maybe he should have gone to the festival, seen if he could track down any allies there. But something odd had happened: he couldn't remember what little town the festival was supposed to take place in. He'd taken everything out of his rucksack, certain that at some point he'd had a flyer for the event. But he couldn't find it, nor remember where he'd been when he'd gotten the flyer. His mind glided away from these questions, drawn back to the problems at hand.

Once again, he'd been walking all day. Hutchins wasn't so big that you couldn't cover the whole town on foot, although almost no one would do such a thing. It was a car town; there were stretches of road where the city planners hadn't bothered to put in any sidewalks, though there was room for them; unbeknownst to Cory or his two companions, Cory had already begun to be remarked upon by motorists who'd passed him more than twice, and he'd been referred to in certain quarters as "the walking guy," or "that homeless-looking kid." If this kept up, he would wind up a staple of the town, a roving landmark.

But it wasn't going to keep up.

Feet sore, legs aching, he turned into Bud's front yard, heading for the back gate. The houses were all so identical that if Bud's car hadn't been in the driveway he would have had to double-check that there were curtains in the windows, to make sure he wasn't wandering into one of the unoccupied houses that flanked it. His eyes flicked around in search of anything spooky. Nothing. He went through the gate and to the deck, where he eased his weary body into one of the lawn chairs.

He sank into it, feeling the pain of so much walking pool up in certain crevices of his body, letting himself relax enough that it could drain out. He stared into space. It would not be right to call what he felt "despair." But he did finally say to himself, *I would give my whole life just to finally see ... you know*—it.

Light began streaking down from the sky. Cory actually rubbed his eyes like a guy in a cartoon—but he knew there was nothing wrong with his eyes. He knew this was a gateway, and his heart banged.

Hands ran down his chest, coming from behind him, on both sides of his neck. Intrigued, he noted the expertness of their touch; they tripped an instant erection. When he turned to look behind him, at the bodies the hands belonged to, they were no longer there. Before he even looked he could sense that they'd moved to over by the pool. For some reason, he wasn't surprised to see that they were the two near-twins from Old Petey's Tavern, the hot girls.

They approached him slowly, but not languorously, and he really couldn't have said what in their body language or cool, flat expressions gave him the conviction that they were coming to fuck him. He wondered who the heck they were, exactly. Or *what* the heck, even.

Without words, without signs, they revealed themselves as the heralds of Amy Madden, come again to Hutchins on the occasion of certain convergences to clear a path for the master they had once trailed through the halls of school. As they plucked clothes from his body and their own, incomplete understanding of them trickled into his mind. No knowledge of their former family life, of the mundane circumstances of their spawning—all that was utterly irrelevant. When Amy Madden had died, they had followed her. They hadn't *died*; they'd only flickered out of this dimension and into another, where they were held in stasis. Once in a while they were put upon the earth, to survey local conditions (the conditions of what, precisely? Cory wasn't able to glean that), and that was why they'd aged since high school; not very often, though, and that was why they'd only aged a bit.

Four nipples feathered his face, hands like lips brushed his cock. That all felt awesome, but Cory nevertheless found the whole situation fascinating enough that he managed to keep part of his mind cool, observant, calm. The faces of the hot girls remained distant and flat; they had been sent to Cory in order that the three of them might create pleasure, but not pleasure for their own enjoyment; rather, pleasure that was to be consumed by Amy Madden, for her own glory and magnification.... Cory directed at the hot girls the thought that all this info was totally fascinating, but what he was really interested in was the nature of Amy Madden herself. Even as the hot girls coaxed and simultaneously stoppered his orgasm by means of amorous techniques beyond his ken, so as to render the ultimate explosion all the more mind-blowing, Cory reminded himself that what he really needed was the dope on Amy Madden. He was supposed to be finding out her true nature, so as to be able to exorcise her and free poor Bud. That was the whole point of his quest.

This time the hot girls responded neither with words nor concepts, but with a kind of vision. He became a floating ethereal eye in a hospital room; through the haze of decades he saw a fucked-up-looking dude in a hospital bed, all taped up and in multiple casts and with his left leg hoisted up in traction. At his bedside, gently snoring, a woman. Even though there was nothing particularly outré about her T-shirt and jeans—the pants weren't, like, crazily flared bell-bottoms, or anything like that—Cory understood that this scene was in the late seventies, early eighties. He sort of wondered who this couple was, but didn't let himself get caught up in the mystery, just tried to keep loose and open to whatever was being revealed.

Now he became aware of some other presence in the room. Like an invisible yellow cloud tracing its way in, nosing through the ajar door, threading through the furniture, passing into the gap between the snoring woman's sprawled knees. Seeping through the denim, then through the cotton of her panties. Soaking through her genitals like water through mud, all the way to her womb.

An incubus, Cory realized. And he understood that this lady was Amy Madden's mom. His gaze passed within the dark spaces of the woman's body; the strange yellow cloud passed through the clutch of eggs held hidden away inside the female, not deigning to take one but sniffing at them, just enough to glean the requisite data, the structural knowledge necessary for its plan. Within the dark wet womb, he saw the spark of the homunculus's formation.

*Where did it come from?* he asked, excited, not even aware of himself asking the question. Obligingly, the hot girls guided him to his answer, even though on the physical plane their faces were still busy around his middle, their fingers in his mouth. His invisible eye jerked out of Mrs. Madden's uterus, was reeled back through the hospital room, away from the guy in traction, through the fluorescent corridors. He found himself face-to-face with a mild-mannered little bald dude with round spectacles, looking wanna-be dapper yet rumpled in an indefinably cute way in his blue suit and polka-dot tie. This guy was dead, Cory was slowly given to realize, despite his beatific smile. He wasn't even a patient. He hadn't even been sick. He'd just wandered in here, sat in this little waiting area, and given up the ghost. Folks would soon start to notice, though no one had yet.

He was evil. Like, fucking *evil*. Understanding penetrated Cory, overrode his low affect, made him shudder, made the building orgasm in his physical body quail and lose a bit of steam. Despite the guy's gentle looks, despite even his lack of earthly crimes, Cory knew that a radical malevolence had dwelt in that skinny chest. And now it had been sent forth, to bring to fruition in Mrs. Madden's womb a more straightforward manifestation. This dude was the incubus, or had been. Amy Madden's true father, or the closest thing to it.

And why? Why reproduce itself in another form this way? Why infect this other couple, why leave its seed cuckoo-fashion in the unsuspecting female? Cory pondered the narrative being presented to him (doing an imperfect job of it, but still a pretty good one, if one considers the vigorous massage and suction

122

being applied, respectively, to his prostate and testicles), but couldn't quite suss out its significance. Maybe it was just the drive to propagate that infects all living things.

Speaking of living things, Cory suddenly suspected he was about to quit being one. Not that he felt any particular menace from the hot heralds—he just had a sudden vibe that the most natural end for this scenario would be him shuffling off the mortal coil. He didn't really mind. The only thing that really bugged him was his quest. It occurred to him that, if he died right away, Sally and Bud would be left without this clue to the ultimate nature of Amy Madden, hence wouldn't be able to use it to figure out how to exorcise her. The knowledge would die with him, sterile.

He tried to rouse himself up out of the hedonistic stupor the hot girls' ministrations had put him into. Tried to get back up to the level of the everyday world. He explained to the hot girls why. Pretty naïve, considering that they were after all the heralds and slaves of Amy Madden. In Cory's defense, he understood perfectly well that he somehow couldn't really hide his aim from the hot girls, and anyway couldn't possibly succeed in extricating himself from them unless they to some degree let him go.

But they did not let him go. The intensity of their ministrations only increased, till he was aware of his far-off body shrieking with pleasure. Soon, he understood, the pleasure would reach such a pitch that it would achieve lift-off, rip itself away from his nerves, and send his spirit careening away from his body, forever and ever.

He tried to hunker far enough back down in reality that he could break free of the hot girls and go around to the front of the house, endure till Sally arrived, tell her what he'd learned. Like she would be able to do much with the knowledge, without his aid—but it was worth a shot—anyway, he knew he didn't have long to live, he knew that the pleasure stoked by the hot girls had burned up too much of his mortal fuel.

He couldn't break free. A few tries, and it became amply clear there was no chance. With relief, he started to let himself slump back down. Giving up was its own pleasure. He settled into the hot girls' guiding hands and guiding spirits, ready enough to let them cast him away. To ease his way, he held the vision of the incubus at the hospital close to his breast. He couldn't pretend it answered *all* his questions. Maybe the info wouldn't even have done Bud and Sally any good, even if he'd stayed alive to transmit it to them. Still, he'd accomplished his life's goal. He'd been granted a moment of revelation.

As he admired the vision of Amy Madden's true nature, the strong-hewed fibers which formed it turned to gossamer. The story began to break apart. Cory stared at the disintegrating wreckage of the narrative, unable to grasp what was happening. Then the full disaster hit him: *This was all bullshit.*

*Yes.* The confirmation came to him from the two hot girls. Along with a bit of glee; not the hot girls' glee, exactly—they merely were the vessels that transmitted it, just as the pleasure they conjured via Cory's body was not truly intended for him or them, but for their master.

This origin story was bullshit. Just a little comic-book something, cobbled up to tease Cory for a few minutes. For the sole purpose of laughing at his outrage when he realized he'd been had. Amy Madden had *not* been conceived by an incubus who'd invaded her putative mother's womb while her "dad" was laid up in the hospital.

So what the fuck was she?

The dark entity laughed at his sudden bewilderment, stronger than ever now that it had been renewed, laughed at his disappointment. She laughed through the vessel of her hot girls; Cory was denied direct access even to her mockery.

No! He tried to shout it, but wherever his mouth was, it had gone slack and drooling. Tried to kick and thrash, but his nerves were too high-singing with pent-up orgasm to transmit any signals to his limbs. No! Fuck you, you bitch! Fuck you, fuck you! That distant laughter grew louder, somehow became overpowering without ever quite manifesting, always hovering just on the verge of his perception. In the physical realm of

Bud's backyard, a few yards above Cory's head and at an angle, a powerful kinetic potentiality began to build. Once Cory was at the height of fury, desperation, and outrage, a far more powerful and savage concoction than any he'd ever before known in his life, that potentiality manifested, and Cory was packed off to some other realm. Maybe to be mounted on a wall, so to speak. Or maybe to nothing at all.

# Sixteen

Sally kept her foot on the accelerator until she got to Bud's house, then skidded to a stop before the curb; the hatchback was lined up crooked, but she put it in park and switched off the ignition anyway. Dusk had turned the sky an ashy blue. Sally snatched her copy of *The Apothecary* as she left the car, slamming the door behind her. Not bothering to lock it. At first she marched straight up the path to the front door, like she was heading for a gunfight in an old Western. Then she thought better of it and veered around to the backyard, to let Cory know what she'd found and see if he had any input.

"Cory!" She didn't try to hide her presence from Bud, or Amy Madden. "Cory!" In fact, as she tramped through the yard to the deck, calling Cory's name, it was like she was trying to provoke Amy Madden into showing herself. Actually, it was exactly like that, and she told herself to cool off and use her head before she got herself killed. Or possessed, or dragged into some hell-dimension to be tortured for a billion years. Problem was, she *wanted* a showdown. Wanted the drama of it. Wanted direct contact with this slippery foe, and with whatever transcendent realm Amy Madden hailed from, contact with that heightened region of reality she couldn't remember having ever dared imagine might really exist, even as a little girl.

"Hey, *Cory!*" She slipped on something, and nearly fell on her ass before managing to dance her balance back. A dark, greasy slick covered the deck chair and the wooden deck surrounding it. Smelled funny, albeit not entirely unpleasant. Sally had a vaguely bad feeling about it. She put the mystery of what it might be out of her mind, and quit calling for Cory.

127

She stood on the deck, staring at the sliding glass door. Now that she'd stopped moving, uncertainty caught up with her. Maybe she should hunt around for someone more qualified. Like, a priest or something. But she didn't believe in that shit. She didn't believe in this shit, either, but at least she didn't have a whole other layer of mumbo-jumbo between her own eyes and whatever was going on.

She had no way of guessing when would be a relatively safe time to talk to Bud. No way to know when Amy Madden kept a lighter grip upon him, if such a time even did exist. So she had no excuse not to just bang on the door and get on with it. And frankly, that suited her right down to the ground. The tension humming within her was mounting to a higher and higher pitch all the time, faster all the time; if she didn't defuse it soon, she'd have a heart attack, or a seizure.

Anyway, that's how it *felt*. But who knew—it might even be true.

First she checked the sliding door: locked. She rapped her knuckles against the glass. "Bud!"

She kept rapping a while, then faltered and stopped. It was silly, but she stopped because she started to feel obnoxious. She waited, shifting her weight uncertainly, listening for the sounds of Bud approaching from within. She hopped and yelped; for an instant she saw, inches away on the other side of the glass, a leering fever-splotched face under a ball cap. Only for an instant. A trick, sent to scare her. Pissed off anew, she rapped on the glass harder than ever. "Hey, *Bud*!"

Now there was noise from within, the distant muffled thumping of someone descending the stairs. Maybe he hadn't heard her earlier, or maybe he'd been hoping she'd go away. Anyhow, nothing had torn him to bits. That was good.

But when he got to the glass separating them his face was pale and lined, eyes red and wide and circled with shadows. In just the past few days he'd lost both weight and hair. "Sally," he said, voice muffled by the glass. She had the unnerving, absurd impression that some of the fear in his eyes was directed at *her*.

128

She waited, and when he didn't go on she said, "Bud, let me in, there's something I need to talk with you about."

His mouth, whose muscles since the haunting had begun had grown lax under thin graying stubble, tightened.

"Come on, Bud," she repeated, trying to coax. "Let me in."

He cleared his throat. "Hey, Sally. I appreciate what you're trying to do here, but this is, you know…. Maybe you ought to just go home, you know? And we can work all this out later."

Out of respect for Bud, and out of embarrassment, she tried not to quite notice the tremble in his voice and the increasing redness of his eyes. "We can't do that, Bud. None of this will go away. We gotta make a stand."

He sputtered out a weak little laugh of disbelief. "Sally, you can't *make a stand* against her. She gets into your head—you can't make a stand against your own head."

"Where's Cory?"

"Usually he just hangs out there in the backyard."

"No, he's not here."

"Well, how should *I* know where he is?!"

Something flickered behind Bud's head. Sally's gaze jumped to the spot: a corner of shadow on the ceiling, leaking into the living room from the kitchen, formed by the wall dividing the two rooms and blocking the illumination from the kitchen's ceiling fixture. Had it stretched out a little, extending its range, sharpening like an arrow? "Hey, Bud. Open the door."

He made a sad and exasperated face, as if there were some important point she stubbornly kept refusing to grasp. "Go home, Sally." But she could tell the face was a put-on. He was hiding his fear from her.

Another flicker in her peripheral vision. Again her eyes sped to the point, locked onto it: another bit of shadow, this time on the floor. Was it only her imagination? Her jumpiness? Were the shadows really encircling Bud? Getting darker? Sharper? "Let me in, Bud."

"To do what?"

"To exorcise her."

"That's *crazy.*" He was begging. "Just, go home! Anyway, isn't Cory the so-called expert on that stuff?"

He must be pretty hot to get rid of her, to insist they wait on Cory's expertise. His naked fear embarrassed her. She resented it; she'd committed to following through with this shit, and if she was going to keep her strength up she would need Bud to remain a person who deserved that sort of commitment. "Cory isn't here right now." She resisted the urge to tell Bud to be a man. Again, she thought she saw something, and again her eyes fixed on the spot too late to be sure. Maybe it was her imagination, but she did believe the room was getting sharper, its shadows sharper. "Bud, it's time. Open the door. I'm not sure, but I think we have to do this together."

"I don't *want* to!" he wailed. "Can't you just go away?!"

It was squealing fear, yes. But the feeling hit her like a slap that it was also more; Bud was a prisoner in this house, sure, and subjected to obscure and perverse torture. But not entirely without complicity. Sally's breath hitched. She didn't know where she was getting her information, but all of a sudden she found herself utterly convinced of its veracity; she couldn't see Bud's experience, couldn't access any of its details, but she could feel what she was sure were its real contours: the impossibly long intervals of nerve-pinching sensations that were probably pain but that the mind could be persuaded to read as pleasure; and more than that, the universe-morphing psychedelic storm of Amy Madden's mind, in which she was able to envelop Bud's smaller, meeker one. *He's gotten addicted to it.* It was like Stockholm Syndrome. Like a satanic blend of DMT and oxycontin. Sally's will had been flagging in the face of Bud's refusal to step up and help, in the face of his cowardly unworthiness. Now a spurt of jealousy and outrage spurred her on; jealousy of Amy Madden, but also jealousy of the fact that only Bud got to fully experience this transformation of the mundane universe. She, too, longed to get close to the horrors of the invading entity, if only so as to know that there were other planes from which one could invade and into which one

130

therefore could also escape; she, too, needed to feel the bland empty universe filled with magic and made anew, and she'd be goddamned if Bud and Amy Madden were going to hog all that shit.

The shadows in the room behind Bud darkened and squirmed. Definitely, this time. Visible to the naked eye, not her imagination. She banged on the glass with both fists. "Bud! Please! Open the door!"

He shook his head, *I'm sorry,* pale, haggard, paler by the second. He took one, two, three steps back. Did he know that he was stepping back into those dark squirming shadows? Was he about to be waylaid by them? Or was he retreating *to* them, and away from her, from all the empty mundane rigmarole she represented?

A shadow lay across her shoulder. It had been there the whole time she'd been standing at the door, but as it darkened and thickened it occurred to Sally that there was nothing overheard blocking any light source in such a way as to cast it. It thickened to the point of a true weighty physical substance, then pulled itself around her neck and yanked her back.

"Sally!" shrieked Bud from somewhere, as the hazy starless night sky reeled before her eyes and the wooden planks of the deck came up to slam against her back. "Sally!" A noise: the glass door opening.

# Seventeen

Almost a year later, Bud and Sally returned to his house from his work picnic at Boonesville Park, wordlessly kicking off their shoes in the foyer, slumping into the living room, slouching onto the sofa. Sally had been working up to say something about Jason Sterne, but sighed and held her tongue as Bud picked the remote up from the side table. She should have said something earlier—she'd had the whole ride home, after all, during which they'd only exchanged monosyllables. If she started talking about heavy stuff now, Bud might think she was just trying to sabotage the TV-watching. She was always complaining about how they watched too much TV, to which Bud always quite reasonably retorted that she was happy enough to watch it once it was on, and was as likely as not to switch it on if he didn't. All true. Sometimes, when it was off, she'd yearn for him to turn it on, straining to send compulsory psychic vibes, so that she'd be able to veg out in front of it, but he'd be responsible.

What petty, pretentious bullshit! She was the worst.

Wasn't like they didn't have anything interesting to talk about. Then again, "interesting" didn't necessarily equate to "pleasant." Every time she saw Jason Sterne (or a hundred other things or people that reminded her of Amy Madden, and that fateful night almost a year ago when they'd fucking vanquished her), it amazed her that she and Bud had ever stopped talking about those days, and especially the events of that particular night; and at the same time she felt more and more at a loss for how to bring it up. That night, after Bud had so bravely flung himself out onto the deck to save her, after they'd enjoined battle against Amy Madden on that half-real psychedelic plane

133

in between universes, they'd come upon Jason Sterne in that blackly empty, harshly lit, sparse world. He'd been naked, spread-eagled upon a giant spiderweb woven of fat, sickly-gray, juicy strands. Ribs showing, belly distended, eyes ringed with shadow dark as kohl, he'd stared at them numbly. His penis, erect, had been a long flesh-colored clarinet wheezing out cracked notes, not particularly musical ones, as if it were the gusting random wind that played them, or one long leaky gasping fart. Bud and Sally had scurried past him, terrified. Never had Sally been clear in her mind whether Jason had actually seen them, through that eerie stoned gaze of his; she didn't know if he'd really been there at all, or if he'd been a mere illusion. And why had his penis been a clarinet? Certainly, whenever they saw him at these excruciating, awkward work functions of Bud's, he never mentioned having encountered them there. Of course, it was the kind of experience you might not want to talk about. The first couple times Sally'd met him, he'd seemed distant, almost traumatized; but that had been not too long after she'd seen his head materialize in a fish tank. Even if that had been a hallucination, he'd definitely barfed the fish up at the office, so *something* had happened to him. But he seemed to have gotten over it. At today's picnic, he'd been positively chatty—with everyone except her and Bud. For the first time, she'd realized that Jason Sterne didn't like Bud. Held him in contempt, as a matter of fact. Weird that she'd never noticed before.

She thought it totally sucked that Bud's job would schedule these employee-bonding things for a Saturday. Shouldn't they at least have the decency to have them during office hours? And give their workers a break? "It's supposed to be for our recreation," Bud had sighed when she'd voiced her objection. "Attendance isn't mandatory." And yet he seemed to think he'd be up shit creek if he skipped one.

The TV blabbered. Sally let her gaze drift along the ceiling. Along the multitudinous but faint shadows of early afternoon with too many lights on. (Not on because anyone feared the dark—they just couldn't be bothered to turn them off.) Sally tried to remember the way the shadows had come to life that night, how they'd moved. She *could* remember, and pretty accurately. But it was like remembering CGI effects from some movie.

The commercials came on. Recently Bud had gotten into the habit of just letting the commercial breaks play out, instead of flipping around for something else to watch during the ads. Sally had always thought she hated when people flipped around during commercials—nobody ever got back to the original program in time, and you wound up watching two or three shows at once and missing big chunks of them. Why couldn't people just show the slightest bit of patience and stick with one thing? Now, though, she found something chillingly lazy about the way Bud just sat there like a lump, gazing at the commercials. How much energy and willpower did it take to just push a button so that you could watch something real, instead of the same old pickup-truck ads?

"Do you think there are people who actually let TV commercials influence which pickup-truck they buy?" she asked, trying to get a conversation going. Bud just grunted.

And then the commercial came on for that fucking show they were making, of the *Apothecary* comics.

The first time they'd seen the ad, last week, Sally had made Bud change the channel. This time she sat through it, feeling her face calcify into something ugly. Her twisting guts were like slugs that had been knotted together too tightly, and now were writhing in salt. Why did it bug her so much that they would make a TV show out of that comic? Well, the comic itself felt like a part of her own personal adventure, her own private trauma. She never would have read it if not for the Amy Madden connection. Well, except now she *would* have read it, because this show looked like it was going to be pretty cool, and she would have read the graphic novels first because she had a neurotic thing about reading source materials before watching TV or cinematic adaptations. Even if Amy Madden had never entered her life, *The Apothecary* would have. That made its connection to those events less particular, less special. It shrank

135

the influence upon her life of this supernatural drama, and her own and Bud's heroic parts in it.

In the storyline of *The Apothecary*, the denizens of the world of Elzwair have the mystical ability to make contact with the world of twenty-first century Earth (which they call Nahwair). Kargloz, the secret prophet of the demoness Amazadan, and apothecary in his day job, is always secretly trying to open a rift between the two worlds so that Amazadan can extend her reign to our world, where she isn't as well-known and guarded against as on her own plane of the multiverse and ergo would find the pickings easy. One of the main tools in his bag of tricks is what he refers to as "alchemy," which has zip to do with actual alchemy, and which basically consists of him taking just about any substance whatsoever and transmuting it into Gold, with a capital G, which differs from regular gold in that it aids in transit across the interdimensional gulfs, and hence could aid Amazadan in her conquest of our world.

When Sally had first read that comic book, heart pounding, palms sweating, remembering her dream of Kargloz, her first thought had been that she must have read this graphic novel before, at some unremembered earlier date, and it must have triggered a psychotic break, spawning weeks' worth of hallucinations. But then she'd come over to Bud's house, and they'd definitely had that interdimensional battle.

Later she'd wondered if *The Apothecary* might itself be some manner of supernatural phenomenon. Maybe it had its true origin on the other side of that interdimensional void its characters were always trying to cross; maybe it was a manifestation, on this side of reality, of some force or entity that couldn't quite appear here in its true shape, and maybe the same was true for Amy Madden, maybe she was in truth a manifestation of Amazadan, that demon with the suspiciously similar name.... But reading the comics, and then the about-the-creators stuff in the back matter, she couldn't buy that. The whole thing just felt too goofy and cobbled-together; the guys who'd written and drawn it just grinned too big in their author photos, they acknowledged the bizarre randomness of their success too gleefully in their self-deprecating bios. *The Apothecary* was plainly a basically ordinary comic book from this plane of existence.

The truth had come to her—not through any process of reasoning, not even through intuition, really, but in a vision. (Not that you can trust those, she reminded herself bitterly.) She saw Amy Madden, a teenager, reading this comic book. Probably she got jazzed by the similarity between her name and the demon Amazadan. And, because Sally really did believe Amy Madden was a supernatural entity of non-human origin, even if she'd accepted that she probably would never learn or comprehend what that entailed, and because she really did believe Amy Madden possessed supernatural powers, regardless of the human form she'd worn, she had a vision of her happening upon this human artifact, this bit of mass-media flotsam, and amusing herself by injecting it with the force of her imagination, with her own soul-stuff. Not enough to make it *really* real. Amy Madden wasn't God, or even *a* god. But enough to flesh it out, to make it the set of her play, the arena of her gladiatorial combat, with folks like Bud cast as the gladiators and Amy Madden herself as the lion.

The commercial was over. Sally felt pummeled by it—she didn't want to move or speak. Yet not to acknowledge the situation felt, somehow, like a shameful defeat. "Wow," she said. "It's crazy that they're coming out with that show."

Bud shrugged.

Sally cleared her throat, feeling embarrassed and stupid even before she spoke, yet unable to stop herself: "You don't suppose.... I mean, I don't guess it's possible that we really *didn't* defeat Amy Madden, is it? Like, this TV show couldn't be a whole new manifestation of her on this, uh, this plane? Plane of existence?"

This time, Bud sighed. "No, I doubt it, Sally. It's probably just a regular TV show, made out of a comic book. They do that all the time."

Sally's embarrassment primed her to get offended. "You don't have to act like it's such a crazy thing to say. I mean, you of all people. After what happened a year ago."

"We'll probably never know what happened a year ago." He flinched under the aghast look she gave him. "Look, I had that beer at the work thing, okay? I should have known better, I should never drink in the hot sun like that, in the middle of the day."

It wasn't even that hot. "You *saved* me a year ago," she said. It sounded like an accusation. "You came right out onto that deck through that sliding door and *saved* me. It was the bravest thing I've ever seen. Probably the *only* brave thing I've ever seen."

"Look, no one is denying that *something* happened. Okay? But I just don't.... I mean, do we have to talk about it every time a new TV show has a commercial?"

"Why the fuck shouldn't we talk about it? Bud, you and I walked through the interdimensional void, or *something*." Saying that out loud embarrassed her, which she resented, because it was true.

"Okay, but I mean ... I mean, do we have to *always* talk about it? You talk about it so much, it's almost like there's nothing else to us *except* that."

That sounded believable; so much so that for a second she nearly bought it, which only made her resent the gambit all the more. The truth was he just didn't want to talk about it.

They hardly ever talked about it, it seemed to her. Not even about Cory's disappearance, not these days. Both family and police had assumed that disappearance was due to some misadventure linked to his peripatetic lifestyle. Even Bud had told Sally that it wouldn't have been all that out of character for Cory to up and take off, without leaving word. Anyway, Bud and Sally couldn't exactly mention Amy Madden to the authorities, so when questioned they'd restricted themselves to the mundane facts, skipping over the supernatural ones. Sally had been alarmed to find that only ever talking about it that way, publicly, had made it difficult to think about it in any other fashion, even in private.

She said, "Can we at least change the channel? To a movie or something? I mean, you have HBO and Showtime and all that. At the very least we could watch something without commercials."

"Sure." Obligingly he flipped to HBO, plainly happy to have something to be obliging about. *Lethal Weapon* was on; Bud turned to her with raised eyebrows and an approval-seeking pout. Sally nodded; she, too, liked *Lethal Weapon*. They settled in to watch Danny Glover and Mel Gibson do battle with evil drug-dealers. Not having any commercial breaks took the pressure off them to talk.

Not that there was a *rule* against talking. After about twenty minutes, Sally said, "You know what I used to wonder, about movies like this, back when I was a kid? In movies like this, so much of the story is about the heroes just not dying. Someone's trying to kill them, and they're trying to escape being killed. But I used to think, Well, who cares? I mean, you're going to die anyway. So what's the big deal? Why should I be invested in whether you die now, because some bad guy killed you, or you die fifteen years from now from, like, cancer or whatever?" She waited, but Bud made no response. Worried she'd unwittingly said something snooty, she hastily added, "I mean, I'm not saying that's bad, I love this movie, I've always loved it. Just, why do we care what happens? From a story-telling perspective. I'm just making conversation."

Without looking away from the screen, Bud gave a slow shrug. "But it's not really about that, though. The real story is about how in the beginning of the movie Mel Gibson is a depressed, self-destructive loser with nothing to live for, and in the course of this big adventure he and Danny Glover have, they become friends. Family, even."

The remark seemed so fucking out-of-the-blue apropos that Sally half-believed there was some sort of supernatural synchronicity thing going on. (Actually, she didn't really half-believe that, but she tried to.) She felt bushwacked. "Yeah, well," she said, spitting out the words, "does shit like *that* ever really happen, in real life?"

Bud stared at her. "What's into you?"

"Nothing." She stood. The sofa was so soft and deep she had to really work to haul herself out of it, which made her feel ridiculous. "I think being out in the sun for that picnic lunch kinda did me in, too. I'm gonna go upstairs and lie down."

# Eighteen

Should have been obvious after that miserable Saturday that they were approaching Break-Upsville.

And maybe it was. Maybe deep down Sally knew, when she told herself they were "working on stuff," that that was her private codeword for "procrastinating." Painful as their life together had suddenly grown, the prospect of ending it was more painful still. Because she'd miss him? Yeah, partly. But better to be honest and admit that it was the finality she really feared. The chopping-off of a segment of experience, which would put her that much closer to the end of that string of segments she called her life. Moreover, this would be yet another segment that ended stagnantly, didn't branch into anything or drop her off someplace new, would just leave her back where she started, waiting for the next damn thing to come along and carry her for a while. She recognized this same old dread from every other relationship she'd ever been in. Good thing she'd never given up her apartment. But she expected her relationship with Bud to just fizzle out pathetically, instead of what ended up happening.

Over the past months, she'd resented Bud more and more for acting like the metaphysical adventures of that night when they'd defeated Amy Madden, flushed her at least temporarily from this plane of existence, had never happened. In truth, though, almost from the very start she'd had trouble shaking the sense that she and he *both* were pretending, right from the moment they'd popped out of that irreal psychedelic starless plane and back onto the rough wood of Bud's deck. She thought often of what Cory had said that one time, about how removing herself from Amy Madden's immediate presence had taken her out of Madden's metaphysical influence, too, causing her mind to resettle into its quotidian metaphysical matrix. That's what seemed to happen as soon as they'd left her realm (or, if not *her* realm, that realm where she'd flourished and they'd floundered, where by rights they ought to have been easy prey for her). Even with the experience of that uncanny non-world still roiling in their minds, even with their nerves still shivering with the adrenaline of the encounter, they'd begun to stop believing in the reality of their own experience. No, not begun, fuck that— they *had* stopped believing, like a switch had been thrown in their brains. Sally could know good and well that Amy Madden really had been haunting Bud, that they really had chased her out of this corner of the psychic cosmos—she could know it, but she couldn't *know*-know it. Because her mind, out of the sphere of influence of Amy Madden and all the weird phenomena surrounding her, reset itself back to its usual operating mode, a mode which simply could not integrate such an experience. It was as if proximity to Madden's world-warping influence had disabled certain key mental antibodies which had kicked back to life once she was gone. She'd discussed all this with Bud, and he'd acknowledged the same strange sense of utterly disbelieving in an experience which he intellectually knew to be real. Fighting off that sense grew harder and harder, till they turned back into just a pair of ordinary, nondescript, mediocre people. Sally assumed that the breakup she could feel impending would take the form of a gradual slackening of the bonds they'd formed, now that the special pressure brought to bear by the haunting wore off and the usual social pressures reestablished hold.

Instead, one day when she was in the bathroom, Bud came knocking on the door. Kind of insistently. "Sally? Hey, Sally?!"

"Yeah, I'll be right there," she said, gritting her teeth. She hated having anyone nearby when she was pooping, especially her boyfriend. She didn't like reminding the person with sexual access to her body just how gross, undignified, and silly it could be. Hesitating, she added, "Anything wrong?" She also hated to ask that, because she didn't like to risk inviting a whole big conversation while she was in this position. But he did sound pretty upset.

"No, I just, uh…." He walked away; she listened to his hasty footsteps, pacing down the hall, turning into the bedroom, then back out and down the stairs. Moving back and forth with restless motion, trying to burn off nervousness. Nervousness about what? Sally welcomed the thrill of fear that came with the thought of those bad old days; hurriedly, she finished her business and cleaned herself up, then rushed out of the bathroom and down the stairs to join Bud. She didn't need anyone to tell her it was nuts to actually hope Amy Madden had reappeared. She knew good and well that if that *did* happen she'd be fucked, and that if the evil specter began torturing her she'd long for these innocent, boring days of not especially believing in anything much. But again, her mere intellectual knowledge of the truth didn't do her much good. She hungered for magic, and from this side of the looking-glass she was willing to pay a hefty price to get it.

She found Bud pacing in the living room. Literally walking in a circle, one hand up and tugging at his thinning hair, the other running its thumb over its fingers again and again, as if compulsively verifying they were still there. "What is it?" demanded Sally, "what happened?" *Game on!* she thought.

His feet stopped but his body kept swaying back and forth, as if it wanted to stay in motion. For a second his stricken eyes met hers, then his face was on the move again, checking the room for some hidden threat. "Listen," he said. "You know how we talked before about how we can't, like, really *believe* in, uh, you know, Amy Madden, now she's gone? Like, about how we actually need her nearby influence in order to even *conceive* of her, and now she's gone we can't?"

Sally nodded. Again, this was a conversation they'd had countless times during those first days after the battle, when the memories of those tortures and perils were fresh but belief in them had flown away.

"Well," said Bud, getting more and more worked up, "I always, all this time, have been saying to myself that it's kind of like that disbelief works in our favor. Like, it lets us go back to our regular lives from before." Gee, what a great goal, said Sally to herself, but held her tongue. "And also, I always kinda tell myself that maybe it can work like sort of an alarm system. Like, we only can believe in Amy Madden when she's nearby. So if we're not believing in her, that must mean she's *not* nearby. Maybe."

"Okay."

"But then I was just thinking, what if we *wouldn't* know? She can do so much. We never understood her, not really. What if she did come back, but somehow kept that mystical field or whatever under control, so that it couldn't influence us after all? So that we didn't believe in her? She could walk right up to the front door and ring the bell! We could open the door and see her there, and yet still not *believe* it! How could we defend ourselves if that happened?!"

"Well, we'd still *know* what she was. We'd know what to do." Actually, that they would know what to do was total bullshit. "Our feelings might tell us that magic and psychic phenomena and all that stuff are unreal, but that doesn't mean we can't use our reason and memories to figure out what the truth really is."

"Yeah, but if she kept us from *really* believing in her, there'd be no *way* we could fight!" He railed that way for almost an hour, pacing jerkily, throwing his arms up, refusing to be calmed. Finally, once he was tired enough, they watched TV for a few hours, then went to bed where he cried himself to sleep. Sally wondered awkwardly, there in the dark beside him, whether she should try to comfort him, or spare his pride by pretending not to notice his weeping. Did he weep such strangled little gasping sobs because he was trying to keep the fit under control, so she wouldn't notice it? Or did he just want her to *think* he was trying to do the manly thing and keep it under control, so that she'd think he'd at least made the effort, and put her hands on him and comfort him?

While he sniffled, and then for a long time after he went to sleep, she replayed the events of that night a year ago in her head—starting with his undeniable bravery. Or, well, "undeniable" was a stupid word, anything could be denied. Still, she felt his bravery had been real.

Even though the action he'd taken on the deck hadn't been anything any corporeal mortal couldn't manage, it had been directed against Amy Madden's supernatural avatars, had interacted with them. And had therefore maybe brought them closer to that liminal zone, where crazy shit became possible, more possible. Sally could remember the triumph with which she'd gasped to Bud, "It all comes down to belief!" (Triumph, but terror too—not that the two were mutually exclusive—in fact it might be that the triumph stemmed from the terror, from the fact that she had ascended to a noncorporeal plane where true terror could flourish—not mere terror of death or physical injury, but terror on behalf of something which might as well be called the soul.) She'd explained to Bud her "theory," which, looking back, hardly deserved the name: how Amy Madden, whatever she might fundamentally be, had *also* been a high school student in Hutchins; how she had stumbled upon the *Apothecary* comic book, and been galvanized, in the mysterious and inexplicable way of all artistic inspiration. Being a supra-earthly creature, Amy Madden's endowment of creative force had been more than earthly. The world of *The Apothecary* served as a mold into which she'd poured this soul-power, fashioning a simulacrum of it advanced enough that one could sort of live in it; one could exile one's victims to it, at least in their dreams; a master could use it for the model of the arena in which its victims would skitter and die.

Mere mortals like Sally and Bud couldn't *really* hope to compete with Amy Madden at that level. They weren't, like, world-makers. "But," Sally had insisted, all that time ago, "we can use the arena she set up. She's built this world, she's set its rules. She can't go against them any more than we can." Of course, the assertion that Amy Madden couldn't break the rules of engagement binding Bud and Sally was ridiculous; at the time, Sally had been convinced of its self-evident truth, but almost as soon as the battle was over she'd realized it had never been more than a vague vibe. Well, maybe it *had* been true; it had fucking worked, right? Maybe the proximity to Amy Madden's weirding influence had helped her see a truth that really *was* self-evident, even if its necessity had since grown obscure to her. Anyway, again, it had worked. Her desperate but close perusal of that graphic novel, and absorption of its world-building, had helped her figure out the strategy they'd used to defeat Amy Madden. The chink in her armor.

The morning after Bud's first freak-out, Sally woke with a violent start. She wasn't aware of any noise or fast movement, or anything else specific that might have awoken her. Bud, in his boxers, was standing stone-still in the corner of the room, hunched over to stare at the corner where the two walls intersected with the carpeted floor, the curve of his hairy back to her. His frozen posture reminded her of a horror movie—the ending of *Blaire Witch Project*, specifically—and her blood flash-froze. *She's here!* "Bud?"

His scurrying feet rotated him a hundred-eighty degrees, like he was voice-activated. His eyes stayed fixed on the floor, didn't look at her. "I just don't *believe* in her!"

Sally sighed—same shit as yesterday. His stricken face frightened and repulsed her; the guilt she felt over her repulsion prompted her to hold her hand out gently and, in her most maternal, melancholy voice, say, "Come back to bed, sweetie."

"But I don't believe in her, or any of it! But it did happen, right?!"

"Yes, it happened. But we talked about this before. We stop being able to believe in all that metaphysically unorthodox stuff once we're out of Amy Madden's influence. So the fact that we have trouble believing that any of it ever happened proves that we won."

"But why can't we believe *at all*?! I *totally* don't believe in her! Is that natural? To totally disbelieve in something that you actually remember going through?"

Sally frowned. "I don't know if I'd say I *totally* don't believe...."

"I totally don't! And that's impossible, because I remember it all! So I ought to believe at least a little bit! So that proves she's still here. She's still exerting some influence on us. Some kind of dampening effect. She's doing it to keep us off our guard, so that when the time comes she'll be able to get us more easily!"

So it went, for days and days. Bud grew more and more terrified that his inability to fully believe in Amy Madden meant she was lurking nearby, biding her time, singling his mind and spirit out for particular attention. Sally couldn't give him much comfort. She tried reasoning with him, but was hampered by the fact that his arguments made a certain cracked sense. Just because they were logical didn't mean they were sane, of course. But even if the arguments were insane, that didn't make them wrong.

More than logic or reasoning, what would help Bud was love. She sensed that. But she couldn't figure out how to get any to him. The fear and increasing hysteria he generated acted like a force-field, evaporating any soft, gentle feelings she could muster. Although she managed, conscientiously, to keep faking them.

"We've got to get away," he croaked one evening, face buried in his hands. On the kitchen table before them were the two boxes of pizza they'd ordered; on their plates were the half-eaten slices. Normally Bud paid for stuff like this, simply because his income was so much laughably higher than hers. But tonight he'd been so distracted that he'd just taken the pizza boxes and forgotten to pay the delivery girl, so Sally'd had to stay behind at the front door, digging through her purse for money. Now she resented him for sabotaging their meal by carrying on his whining here at the table, when she'd just laid out way more money than she could afford. And she felt guilt and self-loathing for her pettiness, when she considered how many thousands of dollars he'd spent on her over the past year.

"Get away, where?" she asked, patiently.

"We just go," he said. "We just drive, until we start believing in her again. And then we'll know we're far enough that we're out of her influence."

"But then what's to stop her from just coming after us again, Bud?" In retrospect, it might have been a better tack to keep attempting to discredit Bud's madness. "Besides, what about our jobs?"

147

"Fuck our jobs! Don't you remember what she could do to us if she caught us? Way worse than kill us!" Sally wondered, in an idle way, whether Bud's inability to quite believe in the sorts of tortures Amy Madden could inflict made them loom that much more horribly in his mind, or whether he was just reacting rationally to memories he knew to be real, even if he could no longer infuse them with vitality. "Anyway, we both hate our jobs! Why would we risk *anything* for them?!"

True. Or, well, no—it was not in fact true that she hated working at Barnes and Noble; only that she yearned to escape it. The same went for Hutchins. She believed she would always retain a warm feeling for the bland, pre-fab, not quite real town, but the fact remained that she'd dreamed of leaving it since she'd been a little girl. Now she arguably had a good reason to get out, and a boyfriend desperate to go and wanting to take her with him. What the heck was stopping her?

At work she became a little less conscientious, and spent a bit more of her time reading on the clock. If the powers that be did get pissed off enough to fire her she'd be able to replace this job pretty easily, with something equally mediocre.

One of the books she spent a stolen half-hour thumbing through claimed that memory never retains physical pain. It can't, it only marks a spot and says *Pain happened here*. Stunned, Sally stared into space, trying to revive within her some sensation of pain. A few times she thought she'd succeeded, but maybe that was only in her imagination (well, except, whether she failed or succeeded, either way it would be "in her imagination").

On a Thursday night she awoke to Bud shaking her shoulder. The dream she'd been in the middle of flitted down the oblivion hole; she almost wanted to pursue it, but, despite having no memory of it, she suspected it hadn't been worth the trouble.

"Sally." Bud's thick gasp sounded as scared as if there had been something dangerous in the house with them. A burglar? But no, she couldn't even bring herself to believe in that.
She sighed. "What is it, Bud?"
"I just feel like we should go?"

"Now? Anyway, go where? You keep saying 'go,' but there's never a plan."

Bud nodded in the dark. She could make out the movement in the gray light. "I don't really have one. It's not the kind of thing you can plan for."

Sally nodded. She knew what he meant. Still, what could she say?

"I just need to go," he said. "Because if I don't, then I'm afraid I'll stop believing any of it ever happened."

They let that sit there between them a moment. Sally supposed maybe he was waiting for an answer. Eventually, she reached down, groped till she found his hand, and clasped it. It felt like the first time in a long while that they'd shared this contact. She said, "If you need to go, then do it."

He waited, not speaking, like he didn't yet quite believe he'd been set free.

"Really," she said. "It's all right."

He squeezed her hand. "I'll always care about you."

"I care about you, too."

Amazingly, they managed to get back to sleep, as if they'd decided nothing very important. In the morning, they shared breakfast, as usual; a little subdued, but nothing odd about that these days. A peck on the cheek apiece, and they parted, Sally off to work. A couple hours into her workday, Bud called her on her iPhone. He explained that he was leaving town in the morning, and would be really busy tonight making arrangements for most of his crap to be sold or put in storage. He spoke in a worried, cautious, experimental tone, as if confirming he had permission. Sally soothed him, reassuring him that she hadn't planned on coming over tonight, anyway.

They hung up amicably. Sally went to straighten some shelves. Less than five minutes later, Bud called again. Kicking himself, calling himself stupid, he apologized to Sally and said it had completely slipped his mind to ask her if she wanted any of his stuff. The big-screen TV? Any of his admittedly scarce books? That recliner she liked? Anything, no big deal, she could come and pick it up, or he could have it shipped to her, or he could even put off leaving town for a day or two if she needed time to go through stuff.… No, no, it was cool. She didn't need anything, for real. Anyway, her apartment didn't have room.

Books weren't likely to spark memories of Bud in the days, weeks, months, years to come. They hadn't exactly sat around reading together. And yet a couple weeks later, as Sally thumbed through books on her shelf to try to distract herself, she did come across *The Hobbit* and it gave her pause.

How funny that she and Bud had that one time talked about the chink in Smaug's scales, and then that remark had turned out to be one of the things that had inspired the plan that had been Amy Madden's downfall. Just luck, obviously. Or maybe some sort of awe-inspiring magical synchronicity. Or possibly evidence that the whole scheme, even the whole struggle, had been a delusion cooked up in her brain by the bits and pieces of crap floating around in there.

Bud's house, she imagined, was all shut up by now. Probably be on the market soon. Bud had up and left his job, so she didn't see any way he could keep up the mortgage. Be hard to unload a house in that neighborhood; after all, almost none of the houses there had ever even been sold a first time. Then again, maybe Bud's would be easier to sell, because it'd been lived in, and therefore ought to be cheaper. Hell, maybe Bud and the realtor had sweetened the deal by throwing in all the furniture and appliances. No way had Bud taken much with him, in that car, and having quit his job how could he pay for storage? She refrained from driving by the house, and she didn't hear from Bud.

Watching *Die Hard* alone one night, with some ice cream and a five-dollar bottle of Riesling, she chuckled at the end, where the main terrorist Alan Rickman has been dispatched and hero Bruce Willis has seemingly saved the day, only to have that crazy henchman pop up all bloody out of nowhere and have to be gunned down: one last surprise baddie, to send you out of the movie on an up note. Action movies almost always had a coda like this.

All sorts of genre films have their little codas. Her smile

faded as she thought of the end of *A Nightmare On Elm Street*. Freddy Kreuger is dead; the dream-world is safe again; our heroine takes refuge there, in her dreams, once more. Her reward for having fought so valiantly. But it's all so saccharine-sweet; the viewer knows things aren't that easy. Suddenly the music turns eerie. The car doors lock, entrapping the heroine's friends. Freddy's rumbling, gobbling laughter echoes through the scene. The last word is reserved for the monster.

Sally swallowed the Riesling, but her mouth still felt dry. These movies always ended like that.

She sat, waiting, unable to help it, craving re-entry to the dream world.

For other works by J. Boyett, please visit

**jboyett.net**

and sign up for the mailing list.

---

J. Boyett can be reached at jboyettjboyett@gmail.com

## ALSO FROM SALTIMBANQUE BOOKS:

**THE SWITCH,** by J. Boyett

Beth used to be a powerful witch, till a meth addiction burned her powers away. Now her daughter Farrah thinks she's nothing but a loser. But Beth thinks maybe Farrah would change her mind if she had to spend a few days in her mom's shoes—and when she gets her hands on a new source of magic, she decides to make that happen....

**IRONHEART,** by J. Boyett

The mining ship *Canary* comes across an ancient derelict on the edge of the galaxy—a derelict occupied by a strange and seemingly immortal woman....

**RAY TAKESHI AND THE MEDALLIONS OF SKARTH,** by J. Boyett

Ray Takeshi doesn't remember his parents—they died in sorcerous battle, when he was just a baby. He's been raised in Missouri by a mage named Ned. Ned says his Destiny approaches: a final test, to determine whether Ray will achieve manhood, or be destroyed.

Just because Ray is a fledgling mage doesn't mean he buys such mumbo-jumbo. But then the delectable succubus Melania von Fleiden shows up in town, alongside her hideous Thrall. Ray has to stop her evil plan—or die trying, at least. Could this be that test Destiny was sending? And if so, does he have the slightest chance of surviving it?

**THE UNKILLABLES,** by J. Boyett

Gash-Eye already thought life was hard, as the Neanderthal slave to a band of Cro-Magnons. Then zombies attacked, wiping out nearly everyone she knows and separating her from the Jaw, her half-breed son. Now she fights to keep the last remnants of her former captors alive. Meanwhile, the Jaw and his father try to survive in a zombie-infested landscape alongside time-travelers from thirty thousand years in the future.... Destined to become a classic in the literature of Zombies vs. Cavemen.

**COLD PLATE SPECIAL,** by Rob Widdicombe

Jarvis Henders has finally hit the beige bottom of his beige life, his law-school dreams in shambles, and every bar singing to him to end his latest streak of sobriety. Instead of falling back off the wagon, he decides to go take his life back from the child molester who stole it. But his journey through the looking glass turns into an adventure where he's too busy trying to guess what will come at him next, to dwell on the ghosts of his past.

**RICKY,** by J. Boyett

Ricky's hoping to begin a new life upon his release from prison; but on his second day out, someone murders his sister. Determined to find her killer, but with no idea how to go about it, Ricky follows a dangerous path, led by clues that may only be in his mind.

**BROTHEL,** by J. Boyett

What to do for kicks if you live in a sleepy college town, and all you need to pass your courses is basic literacy? Well, you could keep up with all the popular TV shows. Or see how much alcohol you can drink without dying. Or spice things up with the occasional hump behind the bushes. And if that's not enough you could start a business....

**I'M YOUR MAN,** by F. Sykes

It's New York in the 1990's, and every week for years Fred has cruised Port Authority for hustlers, living a double life, dreaming of the one perfect boy that he can really love. When he meets Adam, he wonders if he's found that perfect boy after all ... and even though Adam proves to be very imperfect, and very real, Fred's dream is strengthened to the point that he finds it difficult to awaken.

## THE VICTIM (AND OTHER SHORT PLAYS),
by J. Boyett

In *The Victim*, April wants Grace to help her prosecute the guys who raped them years before. The only problem is, Grace doesn't remember things that way.... Also included:

A young man picks up a strange woman in a bar, only to realize she's no stranger after all;

An uptight socialite learns some outrageous truths about her family;

A sister stumbles upon her brother's bizarre sexual rite;

A first date ends in grotesque revelations;

A love potion proves all too effective;

A lesbian wedding is complicated when it turns out one bride's brother used to date the other bride.

## STEWART AND JEAN, by J. Boyett

A blind date between Stewart and Jean explodes into a confrontation from the past when Jean realizes that theirs is not a random meeting at all, but that Stewart is the brother of the man who once tried to rape her.

## THE LITTLE MERMAID: A HORROR STORY,
by J. Boyett

Brenna has an idyllic life with her heroic, dashing, lifeguard boyfriend Mark. She knows it's only natural that other girls should have crushes on the guy. But there's something different about the young girl he's rescued, who seemed to appear in the sea out of nowhere—a young girl with strange powers, and who will stop at nothing to have Mark for herself.

## BENJAMIN GOLDEN DEVILHORNS, by Doug Shields

A collection of stories set in a bizarre, almost believable universe: the lord of cockroaches breathes the same air as a genius teenage girl with a thing for criminals, a ruthless meat tycoon who hasn't figured out that secret gay affairs are best conducted out of town, and a telepathic bowling ball.

**DAUGHTER OF THE DAMNED,** by J. Boyett

Before Carol was born, Harold ruined her mother's life. Now Carol's out for vengeance, with the help of the bounty hunter Snake.

But her quest has set off a trap left by her mother. And Carol and her mother's old enemy will have to team up, if either wants to get out alive.

**THE SEXBOT,** by J. Boyett

The AI Revolution has come, and it ain't easy for a single dad to find a decent job. Most things that a human can do, a computer can do better and cheaper. So Brad provides for his kids as best he can, using virtual reality to remote-control a sexbot in a brothel. Male, female, straight, gay: Brad the anonymous operator does it all. A man's got to provide.

But even the brothel gig is barely enough to scrape by on. So when his kids' guidance counselor Duane shows up as a customer, Brad wonders if he can use this chance encounter to build a better future for his children?

**RAW FLESH, COLD AIR,** by J. Boyett

Eighth-grader Sam Peabody's boyfriend (well, not exactly *boyfriend*) asked her to text him a picture of her boob, so she did. But then her not-really-boyfriend didn't keep it to himself.

So now her life is sorta ruined. But things will get better. After all, the civilized adults charged with Sam's care won't leave her to writhe in hell indefinitely, all on account of a dumb text. Right?

**THE SALTIMBANQUE REVIEW**

After only one issue in 2016, the Saltimbanque Review became defunct! But thanks to the magic of the internet, that one issue is still available (unless you are reading this blurb at some point after the apocalypse, in between scrabbling for grubs under a frigid nuclear sky). Warm the cockles of an old publisher's heart by going online and buying a copy, why don't you? "From Long Island diners to Victorian murderers and small-town French cross-dressers, these writers and poets will transport you as far as the written word can carry you."

www.ingramcontent.com/pod-product-compliance
Lightning Source LLC
Chambersburg PA
CBHW070037260626
47159CB00005B/2064